Y0-BKN-150

```
                      55862
306.85
Hal
Hales, Dianne
The Family
```

Robinson Township Library
Robinson, Illinois 62454

THE
FAMILY

GENERAL EDITORS

Dale C. Garell, M.D.
Medical Director, California Childrens Services, Department of Health Services, County of Los Angeles
Clinical Professor, Department of Pediatrics & Family Medicine, University of Southern California School of Medicine
Associate Visiting Professor, Maternal & Child Health, School of Public Health, University of Hawaii
Former president, Society for Adolescent Medicine

Solomon H. Snyder, M.D.
Distinguished Service Professor of Neuroscience, Pharmacology, and Psychiatry, Johns Hopkins University School of Medicine
Former president, Society of Neuroscience
Albert Lasker Award in Medical Research, 1978

CONSULTING EDITORS

Robert W. Blum, M.D., Ph.D.
Associate Professor, School of Public Health and Department of Pediatrics
Director, Adolescent Health Program, University of Minnesota

Charles E. Irwin, Jr., M.D.
Associate Professor of Pediatrics, Division of Adolescent Medicine, University of California, San Francisco

Lloyd J. Kolbe, Ph.D.
Chief, Office of School Health & Special Projects, Center for Health Promotion & Education, Centers for Disease Control

Jordan J. Popkin
Director, Division of Federal Employee Occupational Health, U.S. Public Health Service

Joseph L. Rauh, M.D.
Professor of Pediatrics and Medicine, Adolescent Medicine, Children's Hospital Medical Center, Cincinnati

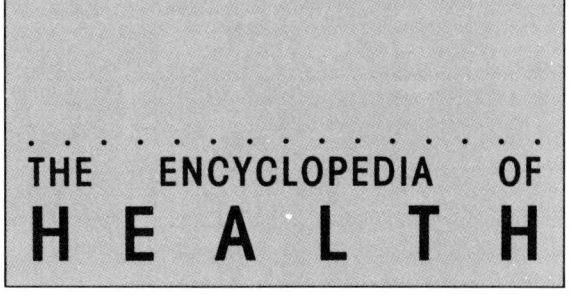

THE LIFE CYCLE
DALE C. GARELL, M.D. · GENERAL EDITOR

THE FAMILY

Dianne Hales

Introduction by C. Everett Koop, M.D., Sc.D.
Surgeon General, U.S. Public Health Service

CHELSEA HOUSE PUBLISHERS
New York · New Haven · Philadelphia

Robinson Township Library
Robinson, Illinois 62454

The goal of the ENCYCLOPEDIA OF HEALTH *is to provide general information in the ever-changing areas of physiology, psychology, and related medical issues. The titles in this series are not intended to take the place of the professional advice of a physician or other health-care professional.*

ON THE COVER *The Hatch Family* (1871) by Eastman Johnson

Chelsea House Publishers
EDITOR-IN-CHIEF: Nancy Toff
EXECUTIVE EDITOR: Remmel T. Nunn
MANAGING EDITOR: Karyn Gullen Browne
COPY CHIEF: Juliann Barbato
PICTURE EDITOR: Adrian G. Allen
ART DIRECTOR: Giannella Garrett
MANUFACTURING MANAGER: Gerald Levine

The Encyclopedia of Health
SENIOR EDITOR: Jane Larkin Crain

Staff for THE FAMILY
ASSISTANT EDITOR: James Cornelius
COPY EDITOR: Richard Fumosa
DEPUTY COPY CHIEF: Ellen Scordato
EDITORIAL ASSISTANTS: Nicole Bowen, Susan DeRosa
PICTURE RESEARCHER: Villette Harris
DESIGNER: Victoria Tomaselli
PRODUCTION COORDINATOR: Joseph Romano

Copyright © 1988 by Chelsea House Publishers, a division of Main Line Book Co. All rights reserved. Printed and bound in the United States of America.

First Printing

1 3 5 7 9 8 6 4 2

Library of Congress Cataloging in Publication Data
Hales, Dianne R., 1950–
  The Family / Dianne Hales.
    p. cm.—(The Encyclopedia of Health)
  Includes index.
  Bibliography: p.
  Summary: Explores the role of the family in society, different types of families, and what constitutes a family in modern and traditional society.
  ISBN 0-7910-0038-9
  1. Family. [1. Family.] I. Title. II. Series.   88-6956
HQ518.H153   1988   CIP
306.8'5—dc19   AC

CONTENTS

Prevention and Education: The Keys to Good Health—
C. Everett Koop, M.D., Sc.D. 7

Foreword—Dale C. Garell, M.D. 11

1 Families Today 13
2 The History of the Family 23
3 Heredity: The Biology of the Family 33
4 The Family Life Cycle 43
5 Family Planning 51
6 All in the Family: Family Dynamics 65
7 Divorce and Single-Parent Families.................... 73
8 Families of the Heart................................. 81
9 Challenges for Today's Families 89
10 Families of the Future 99
Appendix: For More Information 105
Further Reading 108
Glossary 110
Index 114

THE ENCYCLOPEDIA OF HEALTH

THE HEALTHY BODY

The Circulatory System
Dental Health
The Digestive System
The Endocrine System
Exercise
Genetics & Heredity
The Human Body: An Overview
Hygiene
The Immune System
Memory & Learning
The Musculoskeletal System
The Neurological System
Nutrition
The Reproductive System
The Respiratory System
The Senses
Speech & Hearing
Sports Medicine
Vision
Vitamins & Minerals

THE LIFE CYCLE

Adolescence
Adulthood
Aging
Childhood
Death & Dying
The Family
Friendship & Love
Pregnancy & Birth

MEDICAL ISSUES

Careers in Health Care
Environmental Health
Folk Medicine
Health Care Delivery
Holistic Medicine
Medical Ethics
Medical Fakes & Frauds
Medical Technology
Medicine & the Law
Occupational Health
Public Health

PSYCHOLOGICAL DISORDERS AND THEIR TREATMENT

Anxiety & Phobias
Child Abuse
Compulsive Behavior
Delinquency & Criminal Behavior
Depression
Diagnosing & Treating Mental Illness
Eating Habits & Disorders
Learning Disabilities
Mental Retardation
Personality Disorders
Schizophrenia
Stress Management
Suicide

MEDICAL DISORDERS AND THEIR TREATMENT

AIDS
Allergies
Alzheimer's Disease
Arthritis
Birth Defects
Cancer
The Common Cold
Diabetes
Drugs: Prescription & OTC
First Aid & Emergency Medicine
Gynecological Disorders
Headaches
The Hospital
Kidney Disorders
Medical Diagnosis
The Mind-Body Connection
Mononucleosis & Other Infectious Diseases
Nuclear Medicine
Organ Transplants
Pain
Physical Handicaps
Poisons & Toxins
Sexually Transmitted Diseases
Skin Diseases
Stroke & Heart Disease
Substance Abuse
Tropical Medicine

PREVENTION AND EDUCATION: THE KEYS TO GOOD HEALTH

C. Everett Koop, M.D., Sc.D.
Surgeon General,
U.S. Public Health Service

The issue of health education has received particular attention in recent years because of the presence of AIDS in the news. But our response to this particular tragedy points up a number of broader issues that doctors, public health officials, educators, and the public face. In particular, it points up the necessity for sound health education for citizens of all ages.

Over the past 25 years this country has been able to bring about dramatic declines in the death rates for heart disease, stroke, accidents, and, for people under the age of 45, cancer. Today, Americans generally eat better and take better care of themselves than ever before. Thus, with the help of modern science and technology, they have a better chance of surviving serious—even catastrophic—illnesses. That's the good news.

But, like every phonograph record, there's a flip side, and one with special significance for young adults. According to a report issued in 1979 by Dr. Julius Richmond, my predecessor as Surgeon General, Americans aged 15 to 24 had a higher death rate in 1979 than they did 20 years earlier. The causes: violent death and injury, alcohol and drug abuse, unwanted pregnancies, and sexually transmitted diseases. Adolescents are particularly vulnerable, because they are beginning to explore their own sexuality and perhaps to experiment with drugs. The need for educating young people is critical, and the price of neglect is high.

Yet even for the population as a whole, our health is still far from what it could be. Why? A 1974 Canadian government report attributed all death and disease to four broad elements: inadequacies in the health-care system, behavioral factors or unhealthy life-styles, environmental hazards, and human biological factors.

To be sure, there are diseases that are still beyond the control of even our advanced medical knowledge and techniques. And despite yearnings that are as old as the human race itself, there is no "fountain of youth" to ward off aging and death. Still, there is a solution to many of the problems that undermine sound health. In a word, that solution is prevention. Prevention, which includes health promotion and education, saves lives, improves the quality of life, and, in the long run, saves money.

In the United States, organized public health activities and preventive medicine have a long history. Important milestones include the improvement of sanitary procedures and the development of pasteurized milk in the late 19th century, and the introduction in the mid-20th century of effective vaccines against polio, measles, German measles, mumps, and other once-rampant diseases. Internationally, organized public health efforts began on a wide-scale basis with the International Sanitary Conference of 1851, to which 12 nations sent representatives. The World Health Organization, founded in 1948, continues these efforts under the aegis of the United Nations, with particular emphasis on combatting communicable diseases and the training of health-care workers.

But despite these accomplishments, much remains to be done in the field of prevention. For too long, we have had a medical care system that is science- and technology-based, focused, essentially, on illness and mortality. It is now patently obvious that both the social and the economic costs of such a system are becoming insupportable.

Implementing prevention—and its corollaries, health education and promotion—is the job of several groups of people:

First, the medical and scientific professions need to continue basic scientific research, and here we are making considerable progress. But increased concern with prevention will also have a decided impact on how primary-care doctors practice medicine. With a shift to health-based rather than morbidity-based medicine, the role of the "new physician" will include a healthy dose of patient education.

Second, practitioners of the social and behavioral sciences—psychologists, economists, city planners—along with lawyers, business leaders, and government officials—must solve the practical and ethical dilemmas confronting us: poverty, crime, civil rights, literacy, education, employment, housing, sanitation, environmental protection, health care delivery systems, and so forth. All of these issues affect public health.

Introduction

Third is the public at large. We'll consider that very important group in a moment.

Fourth, and the linchpin in this effort, is the public health profession—doctors, epidemiologists, teachers—who must harness the professional expertise of the first two groups and the common sense and cooperation of the third, the public. They must define the problems statistically and qualitatively and then help us set priorities for finding the solutions.

To a very large extent, improving those statistics is the responsibility of every individual. So let's consider more specifically what the role of the individual should be and why health education is so important to that role. First, and most obviously, individuals can protect themselves from illness and injury and thus minimize their need for professional medical care. They can eat a nutritious diet, get adequate exercise, avoid tobacco, alcohol, and drugs, and take prudent steps to avoid accidents. The proverbial "apple a day keeps the doctor away" is not so far from the truth, after all.

Second, individuals should actively participate in their own medical care. They should schedule regular medical and dental checkups. Should they develop an illness or injury, they should know when to treat themselves and when to seek professional help. To gain the maximum benefit from any medical treatment that they do require, individuals must become partners in that treatment. For instance, they should understand the effects and side effects of medications. I counsel young physicians that there is no such thing as too much information when talking with patients. But the corollary is the patient must know enough about the nuts and bolts of the healing process to understand what the doctor is telling him. That is at least partially the patient's responsibility.

Education is equally necessary for us to understand the ethical and public policy issues in health care today. Sometimes individuals will encounter these issues in making decisions about their own treatment or that of family members. Other citizens may encounter them as jurors in medical malpractice cases. But we all become involved, indirectly, when we elect our public officials, from school board members to the president. Should surrogate parenting be legal? To what extent is drug testing desirable, legal, or necessary? Should there be public funding for family planning, hospitals, various types of medical research, and medical care for the indigent? How should we allocate scant technological resources, such as kidney dialysis and organ transplants? What is the proper role of government in protecting the rights of patients?

What are the broad goals of public health in the United States today? In 1980, the Public Health Service issued a report aptly entitled *Promoting Health-Preventing Disease: Objectives for the Nation.* This report expressed its goals in terms of mortality and in terms of intermediate goals in education and health improvement. It identified 15 major concerns: controlling high blood pressure; improving family planning; improving pregnancy care and infant health; increasing the rate of immunization; controlling sexually transmitted diseases; controlling the presence of toxic agents and radiation in the environment; improving occupational safety and health; preventing accidents; promoting water fluoridation and dental health; controlling infectious diseases; decreasing smoking; decreasing alcohol and drug abuse; improving nutrition; promoting physical fitness and exercise; and controlling stress and violent behavior.

For healthy adolescents and young adults (ages 15 to 24), the specific goal was a 20% reduction in deaths, with a special focus on motor vehicle injuries and alcohol and drug abuse. For adults (ages 25 to 64), the aim was 25% fewer deaths, with a concentration on heart attacks, strokes, and cancers.

Smoking is perhaps the best example of how individual behavior can have a direct impact on health. Today cigarette smoking is recognized as the most important single preventable cause of death in our society. It is responsible for more cancers and more cancer deaths than any other known agent; is a prime risk factor for heart and blood vessel disease, chronic bronchitis, and emphysema; and is a frequent cause of complications in pregnancies and of babies born prematurely, underweight, or with potentially fatal respiratory and cardiovascular problems.

Since the release of the Surgeon General's first report on smoking in 1964, the proportion of adult smokers has declined substantially, from 43% in 1965 to 30.5% in 1985. Since 1965, 37 million people have quit smoking. Although there is still much work to be done if we are to become a "smoke-free society," it is heartening to note that public health and public education efforts—such as warnings on cigarette packages and bans on broadcast advertising—have already had significant effects.

In 1835, Alexis de Tocqueville, a French visitor to America, wrote, "In America the passion for physical well-being is general." Today, as then, health and fitness are front-page items. But with the greater scientific and technological resources now available to us, we are in a far stronger position to make good health care available to everyone. And with the greater technological threats to us as we approach the 21st century, the need to do so is more urgent than ever before. Comprehensive information about basic biology, preventive medicine, medical and surgical treatments, and related ethical and public policy issues can help you arm yourself with the knowledge you need to be healthy throughout your life.

FOREWORD

Dale C. Garell, M.D.

Advances in our understanding of health and disease during the 20th century have been truly remarkable. Indeed, it could be argued that modern health care is one of the greatest accomplishments in all of human history. In the early 1900s, improvements in sanitation, water treatment, and sewage disposal reduced death rates and increased longevity. Previously untreatable illnesses can now be managed with antibiotics, immunizations, and modern surgical techniques. Discoveries in the fields of immunology, genetic diagnosis, and organ transplantation are revolutionizing the prevention and treatment of disease. Modern medicine is even making inroads against cancer and heart disease, two of the leading causes of death in the United States.

Although there is much to be proud of, medicine continues to face enormous challenges. Science has vanquished diseases such as smallpox and polio, but new killers, most notably AIDS, confront us. Moreover, we now victimize ourselves with what some have called "diseases of choice," or those brought on by drug and alcohol abuse, bad eating habits, and mismanagement of the stresses and strains of contemporary life. The very technology that is doing so much to prolong life has brought with it previously unimaginable ethical dilemmas related to issues of death and dying. The rising cost of health-care is a matter of central concern to us all. And violence in the form of automobile accidents, homicide, and suicide remain the major killers of young adults.

In the past, most people were content to leave health care and medical treatment in the hands of professionals. But since the 1960s, the consumer of medical care—that is, the patient—has assumed an increasingly central role in the management of his or her own health. There has also been a new emphasis placed on prevention: People are recognizing that their own actions can help prevent many of the conditions that have caused death and disease in the past. This accounts for the growing commitment to good nutrition and regular exercise, for the fact that more and more people are choosing not to smoke, and for a new moderation in people's drinking habits.

People want to know more about themselves and their own health. They are curious about their body: its anatomy, physiology, and biochemistry. They want to keep up with rapidly evolving medical technologies and procedures. They are willing to educate themselves about common disorders and diseases so that they can be full partners in their own health-care.

The ENCYCLOPEDIA OF HEALTH is designed to provide the basic knowledge that readers will need if they are to take significant responsibility for their own health. It is also meant to serve as a frame of reference for further study and exploration. The ENCYCLOPEDIA is divided into five subsections: The Healthy Body; The Life Cycle; Medical Disorders & Their Treatment; Psychological Disorders & Their Treatment; and Medical Issues. For each topic covered by the ENCYCLOPEDIA, we present the essential facts about the relevant biology; the symptoms, diagnosis, and treatment of common diseases and disorders; and ways in which you can prevent or reduce the severity of health problems when that is possible. The ENCYCLOPEDIA also projects what may lie ahead in the way of future treatment or prevention strategies.

The broad range of topics and issues covered in the ENCYCLOPEDIA reflects the fact that human health encompasses physical, psychological, social, environmental, and spiritual well-being. Just as the mind and the body are inextricably linked, so, too, is the individual an integral part of the wider world that comprises his or her family, society, and environment. To discuss health in its broadest aspect it is necessary to explore the many ways in which it is connected to such fields as law, social science, public policy, economics, and even religion. And so, the ENCYCLOPEDIA is meant to be a bridge between science, medical technology, the world at large, and you. I hope that it will inspire you to pursue in greater depth particular areas of interest, and that you will take advantage of the suggestions for further reading and the lists of resources and organizations that can provide additional information.

• • • •

CHAPTER 1

FAMILIES TODAY

There has never been one universal pattern for families. Americans think of family as everyone linked by marriage or blood. In some cultures, all the members of one community see themselves as related. In other cultures, the family extends across place and time, to all the remembered generations of ancestors and to all the generations of children yet to be born.

Yet we are all family: Everyone is someone's daughter or son, and many of us are also brothers or sisters. Eventually most of us will become wives or husbands—and perhaps mothers or fathers, too.

THE FAMILY

Beyond these fundamental roles, we are grandchildren, nieces, nephews, cousins, uncles, aunts. Such relationships tie us to the past and the future, to all who have come before and all who may come after. They define our place in time in the world.

For all of human history, people have come together to live and work. Something within us then reaches out to forge bonds of blood, love, and loyalty with others, and those bonds are enduring enough that families have survived wars, epidemics, and natural catastrophes. As the anthropologist Margaret Mead once put it, families are "the toughest institution we have."

WHAT IS A FAMILY?

A definition of the traditional family is any group of people united by marriage, blood, or adoption, constituting a single household, interacting and communicating with each other, and creating and maintaining a common culture. Some contemporary sociologists have broadened the definition to include people who may or may not be related, who live together only part of their lives,

The nuclear family, once by far the most common structure in America, is gradually giving way to a variety of different household arrangements.

Families Today

"Home" once meant a place for kin of three or four generations. But the same sentiment now applies just as surely to the many different types of families found in society today.

who work together to satisfy emotional needs, and who relate to each other to fulfill wants.

The U.S. Census Bureau's definition is simpler. In its eyes, a family is "a group of two or more persons who are related by blood, marriage, or adoption and [who are] residing together."

In our society, the best-known family type is the *nuclear family*, which consists of members of two generations: two parents and a child or children, a single parent and a child or children, a couple with several adopted or foster children.

Extended families include relatives other than parents and children, such as grandparents or cousins. A family that is nuclear most of the time may become extended in times of illness or economic setbacks when relatives move in.

Conjugal families are extended families in which closely knit relatives live in the same geographic area but not in the same household. Relying on modern communications and transportation, even family members who live far from each other can maintain close conjugal ties.

The family you are born into is your *family of orientation*; the family you form by marriage is your *family of procreation*. Traditionally, each marriage has heralded the birth of a new family. But the lack of a marriage certificate does not mean a family cannot or will not be formed.

A *single-parent family* is headed by one parent who has never married or who is left alone after a death, divorce, or desertion. This type of family is increasingly common in America, and though its members may suffer the absence of a second parent they can also know a closeness or tightness that benefits them as well.

THE FAMILY

Reconstituted or *blended families* are formed after at least one spouse has ended a previous marriage and then entered the current one. Usually these families include children from a previous marriage. This kind of household arrangement is also on the rise.

What Makes Families Different—and Alike?

Throughout most of history, families have been *patriarchal*, vesting the great majority of their power and authority in fathers. This arrangement was typical of the ancient Hebrews, Greeks, and Romans; it remains true in many cultures around the world today. There have also been partially *matriarchal* societies, in which mothers and other women are the community leaders, though no pure matriarchy is thought to have existed. Various African and Indonesian peoples have observed forms of female primacy, and some American Indian tribes, notably the Iroquois, were matrilineal (the husband goes to live with the wife's family, and the children's heritage is traced through maternal lines).

In recent decades Americans and other people of the developed world have begun moving toward an *egalitarian* family form, which distributes power equally between husbands and wives. On the other end of the spectrum, the women of some poorer countries in Africa and Latin America do most of the physical and agricultural labor although the men continue to hold all authority in the family and the community.

One of the key influences on families is *ethnicity*, the unique characteristics of a cultural subgroup. Our ethnic backgrounds may determine part of how we think, work, relax, celebrate holidays, express anxiety, feel about life and death, and establish personal values. Since around World War II, the nuclear family has been the home base of most white Americans, whereas black American families have tended to keep the old-time extended or conjugal form, with many ties to relatives and community members. And Chinese or Japanese families living in the United States, for example, are two or three times more likely than Irish- or German-descended families to be extended, with aged relatives living alongside younger generations. This statistic may have more to do with the comparatively recent arrival in America of the Asian people than with any inherent cultural trait, for family style cannot be predicted solely on the basis of ethnicity.

Regardless of ethnic origins, all families in all societies have shared two common characteristics: recognition of legitimacy and a ban on incest (sexual relations between close relatives).

According to the principle of legitimacy, children born to a married couple have certain rights (including the right to inherit their property), and the husband, whether or not he is the biological father, serves as their protector, guardian, and link to society. Even when they do not discriminate against illegitimate children (those born out of wedlock), all cultures at least note the distinction between legitimate and illegitimate children.

Every society also has rules against sexual relations between close relatives, although some permit sex between cousins and others do not. Procreation among closely related people often results in such birth defects as mental retardation, and it increases the risk that a minor or *recessive* genetic trait—one that would normally be offset by a mate's *dominant* gene—will be inherited by the couple's children. (Genetics are explained more

More couples are choosing not to have children. Many believe that this increases their chances of having an egalitarian or equal partnership.

THE FAMILY

fully in Chapter 3.) Hemophilia, a condition that delays the blood's clotting process, is one such recessive trait. The Romanov house of Russia, rulers for 300 years, produced more hemophiliac males than average because of frequent marriage between close relatives who carried the recessive gene for hemophilia.

But even before they had a scientific knowledge of genetics, societies made incest a taboo. The consequent birth defects and perhaps an innate sense that it was unhealthy were among the possible reasons.

The Functions of the Family

Families can be defined by what they do as well as what they are. Sociologists have identified several key functions that modern families fulfill:

- Regulation of sexual behavior and reproduction: The basic purpose of families is to assure the survival of the human species by producing new members. The family, as a social institution, provides security and stability so two people can establish an intimate relationship and conceive and bring up children.

- Socialization: The family is a training ground for living. Parents are responsible for teaching children the ways of their world, from such fundamentals as toilet training to a sophisticated grasp of unspoken social rules. We use our early experience in our homes to learn how to behave in other places with other groups.

- Protection and personal security: The family provides a safe environment for the most vulnerable members of any society—children, the ill, and, in many countries, the elderly. Most people also look to the family for the unconditional emotional acceptance that provides the basis for psychological well-being.

- Emotional expression: Love is the reason most men and women marry, have children, and form families. Whereas we must sometimes play certain roles at school or work, at home with our families we are free to be ourselves, to communicate our feelings, to forge the most intimate of bonds.

- Providing satisfaction and a sense of purpose: Work is rarely gratifying at all times, even for those in challeng-

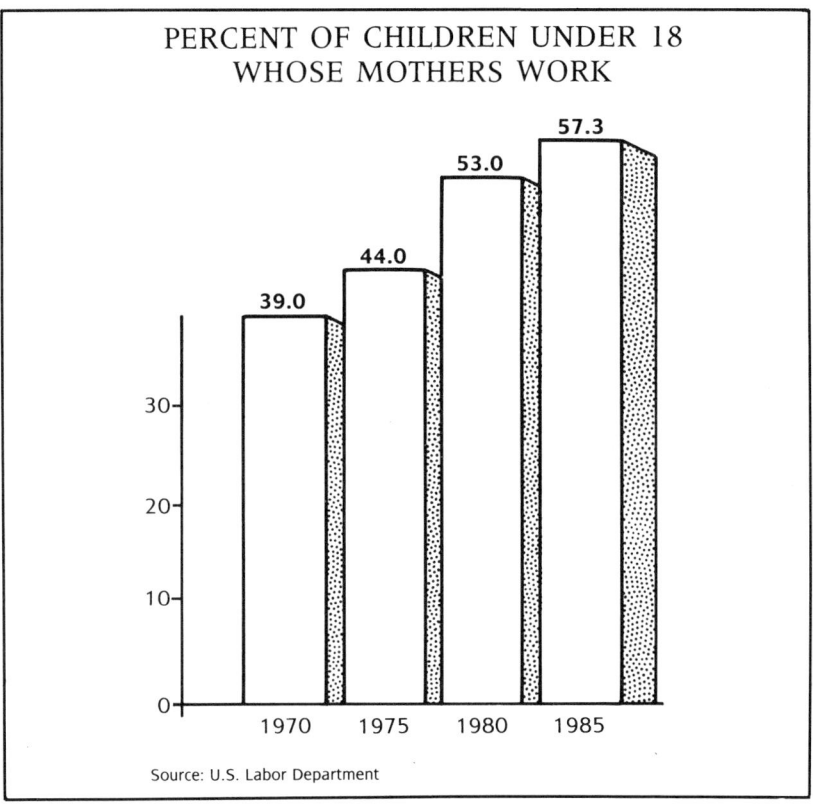

Since the 1960s, the greater number of working mothers has meant changes in the makeup of many households. The trend in the near future seems to be that even more women will join the work force.

ing careers. Most people receive their greatest emotional fulfillment through family gatherings, celebrations, rituals, and tradition.

- Conferring of status: In the past, the family defined an infant's place in society. Today the family continues to teach children what is expected of them and how they may fit into society.

- Developing values: Children learn many of the rules, responsibilities, and obligations of society (and may reject what they learn) from their families. The praise and punishment they receive in their earliest years instill in them the sense of right and wrong that may carry them into adulthood. Surveys have found that many leading student protesters of the 1960s and early 1970s were the children of activist parents and that the "generation gap" made so much of by the public was not as big within most families as many people thought.

THE FAMILY

Family Behavior There are perhaps as many theories of family behavior as there are families. Because each person within each group will act differently, the dynamics are hard to pinpoint and summarize. Some families are ruled by one person, some by two, and some seem to have no focus or direction, which can be either a good or bad thing depending on everyone's needs. And some are abusive. It is estimated that one in every three or four families includes a physically abused member, usually the wife or a child.

Psychological abuse is harder to quantify and therefore does not lend itself to the design of an appropriate therapy. A whole field of family therapy has arisen in the past two decades, involving social workers and specialists in mental health and group interaction. Psychological trouble for one member may indicate that physical violence is on the way, so it is best to try to stem the problem before it worsens. For a distressed family, the most difficult part of therapy is simply admitting that one or more members need outside help.

A family in which both parents work can provide a healthy model for the children, who learn many of their values from their elders.

THE CHANGING FAMILY

The traditional nuclear family structure—father as sole wage earner, mother as full-time homemaker, children all living under the same roof—is now the practice of only about 11% of all American families. And fewer than 30% of all households in the country consist of a married couple with children. The other 70% are the divorced, the elderly, and the single.

The nuclear family is not obsolete; it is simply no longer the primary living arrangement. And even though fewer people choose marriage now than 20 years ago, marriage itself has not gone out of style. The vast majority of Americans (96 of every 100) still marry; almost two-thirds remain married until parted by death. After doubling from 1965 to 1985, the divorce rate is holding steady, and experts predict a slight decline. Of the 38% of couples who get divorced, 75% of the women and 83% of the men remarry within 3 years.

Yet there are changes under way. Largely because of divorce, the number of single-parent families has jumped from 11% in 1975 to 21% today. Among the problems single-parent families face are economic strain, the need for one parent to play the dual roles of father and mother, and pressure on the children to take on responsibilities for which they may not be ready.

When divorced men and women remarry, they bring their children together to merge into stepfamilies or blended families. More than 35 million adults are stepparents; 1 in every 4 children is a stepchild. All face the challenges of finding new ways to relate to each other as they come together to function as a family.

Even in the conventional nuclear family, dramatic changes have taken place. More than half of wives and mothers now work. Nearly 6 out of 10 children have mothers who work, compared to 4 out of 10 in 1970. The demands of dual careers have forced men and women to rethink and renegotiate roles and responsibilities.

In the future, families may take on even more varied forms. More women are having children without marrying; more gay male and lesbian couples are setting up households, and some are having children through adoption and artificial insemination; more Americans are living alone; more couples are remaining childless.

Such variations in family arrangements are not necessarily new. Rather, they reflect a society more open, more tolerant of social change and of individual preferences. Most sociologists—scientists who study the structures of society—agree that what we are witnessing is not a fragmentation of traditional family patterns, but the emergence of greater acceptance of variety in family living arrangements.

•   •   •   •

CHAPTER 2

THE HISTORY OF THE FAMILY

Nebraska family, 1880s

In prehistoric times, families had only two basic functions: survival and reproduction. Life was harsh, dangerous, and short, and our earliest ancestors left no written record of their family structure. The first families recorded in history, the Hebrews, lived almost 4,000 years ago in the area we now call the Middle East.

The Hebrews were nomads who roamed the countryside seeking pasture for their animal herds and living with an elaborate kinship system. Each family belonged to a "sib," a group of kinsmen related through the husbands and fathers, and a clan, which included wives as well. Several related clans made up a tribe.

THE FAMILY

Society in ancient Greece was patriarchal, with all authority and power vested in men. The system included a father's option of choosing a husband for his daughter.

Hebrew society gave nearly absolute power to the father of the family. Fathers had complete control over their children and could even put them to death—legally—if they were persistently disobedient. Marriages were often arranged to create or strengthen bonds between two extended families; wives were treated as property.

Wealthy Hebrew men had several wives, as well as concubines (sexual partners to whom they were not married) in their homes. One rationalization for this polygamy—a man having more than one wife—was the high value placed on sons. A barren wife, one unable to bear children, might even give her female servant to her husband as a concubine and claim the children as her own.

Ancient Greeks Greece in the 500 years before Christ was the world's dominant power, and an agricultural country of strong patriarchal families. Extended families belonged to a "gens," a clan made up of families who traced descent from a common ancestor.

The Greek father, like the Hebrew father, was extremely powerful, both as trustee of the family estate and as priest in the worship of ancestors. Only men could carry on worship of the ancestors; women were treated as inferiors, having been given a poor education and no legal rights.

The History of the Family

Fathers could decide whether an infant should be left to die (a fate that befell mainly the sick, deformed, or illegitimate children, particularly girls). Fathers could also sell children into servitude and arrange their marriages.

The Greeks prized marriage, which was considered a sacred obligation. Both Athens and Sparta, the primary cities, passed laws punishing those who remained single. The Greeks were monogamous (having only one legal wife), but, like the Hebrews, often kept concubines.

Roman Families During the century before the birth of Christ, the power of Greece gave way to the increasing power of the Romans. The early Roman family was the strongest patriarchy in history, with large, stable families totally controlled by the father. He could sell his children into slavery, banish them, or marry them off against their will. And his power lasted as long as he lived; not even grown sons could control their own property or earnings.

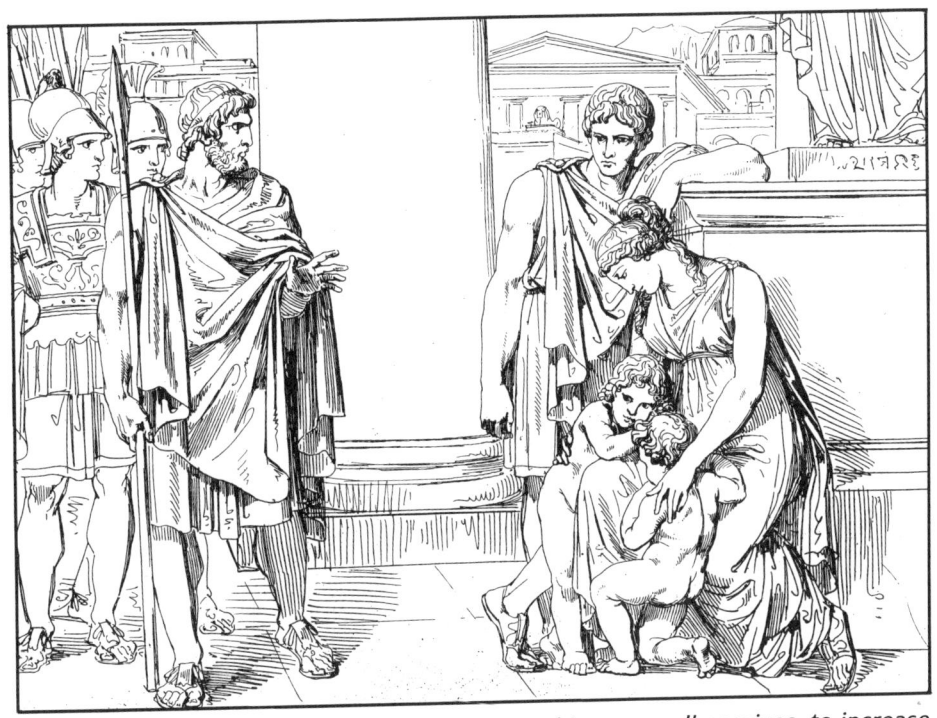

Wealthy men in ancient times often kept concubines as well as wives, to increase their chances of having male heirs. Over the centuries, women gradually gained the right to choose their own spouse.

THE FAMILY

Marriage was seen as a patriotic and religious duty. Women had no legal standing, yet Roman wives had high social status, were educated, and were treated as respected mistresses of their households.

Over the next few centuries, Roman families changed, with a decline in the once-absolute power of the father. In the highest economic classes, men and women stopped marrying out of obligation and began taking mates of their personal choice. Some did not marry at all. The birthrate began to fall, despite laws heavily taxing the estates of childless couples. Divorce also became common, including divorce by mutual consent.

The Families of Europe With the fall of the Roman Empire in the 5th century, loosely united tribes of barbarians swept through the countryside, leaving few records of their families. As the tribes were continually at war, kinship to them meant individual protection. If a man were killed, his kin avenged him or extracted payment from the slayer's kin.

By the late Middle Ages, marriages in most European countries were more a matter of business than romance. Parents pledged their children, even as infants, as future partners. The groom's father agreed to give the bride's father cattle, money, or arms and offered a sort of deposit at the time of the betrothal. Eventually the payment went directly to the bride; much later the payment took the form of a ring—an early form of today's wedding ring.

Again, fathers dominated families, and sons were highly valued. Most estates were left to just one son, usually the eldest, the younger sons having to fend for themselves. Wives could do nothing on their own; their function was to provide heirs.

Some time after the year 1500, the extended family gradually began to give way to the nuclear family. Both the Roman Catholic and Protestant churches began to promote the ideal of a family born of love, not economics. And whereas society in the past could hold an entire family responsible for an individual's crimes, philosophers now began to recognize each person's own accountability under God. The law began to hold only the perpetrator responsible. This shift was a part of the movement away from the extended family's importance, with individuals more free to pursue their own goals and more responsible for their actions.

The History of the Family

China's population of more than one billion (more than a fifth of the earth's people) has led its government to legislate in favor of one-child families.

Chinese Families Because of its vast population and long history, China can claim more families than any other nation. A majority of its people still work the land, their isolation and the hardships of a life based on the whims of nature forcing them into family patterns common to less developed societies. Everyone works; physical survival is their first goal and concern.

In China, the "gentry" (property owners and intellectuals) formed family units that persisted for 2,000 years relatively unchanged. The traditional Chinese family was patriarchal and included the father and his wife, their sons and their wives, unmarried daughters, grandsons and their wives, unmarried granddaughters, great-grandsons and their wives, and so on down the line of genetic descent.

The ideal was to have six generations living under one roof. In reality, two or three generations were probably most common, and usually only one son would bring his wife into the family home, maintain the family burial ground, and continue ancestor worship.

THE FAMILY

Beyond the extended family was the clan, or *tsu*, which included all persons with a common surname tracing descent from a common ancestor. In some parts of the country, entire villages belonged to the same tsu.

Children were highly valued, especially boys. Men took only one wife but usually had concubines and could divorce wives who were disobedient, barren, adulterous, severely diseased, jealous, too talkative, or dishonest. Still, divorce was rare.

A new family form emerged in the late 1800s as China began to industrialize and establish contacts with the West. With the growth of cities and factories, single people, married couples, and nuclear families could break away and support themselves.

This independence undermined parental authority. For the first time, women became potential sources of income, although males continued as the favored sex. Though marriages were still arranged at times, parents began asking their children's consent. Sometimes children found their own mates and asked for parental approval.

In 1949, Mao Zedong led a revolutionary communist rebellion that took control of China. Eight months later the government issued a marriage law establishing certain principles, including monogamy (one wife per man), a ban on arranged marriages, equal inheritance rights, protection of children's rights, and divorce by mutual consent as well as a woman's right to initiate one.

Communism broke up the tsus by redistributing land to the peasants. Agricultural cooperatives, set up to nationalize farm production in the 1950s, failed, and gave way to communes of about 5,000 families each. These communes took over many functions of the family, providing nurseries and dining rooms, for instance. In 1985, each rural commune was divided roughly in half for easier management, and the new unit was called a township. (Urban areas were divided into what are called workers' residential areas.) Central planning for the economy has given way in part to some free-market practices, though the collectives still play a dominant role in social and family care.

In the interest of population control, the Chinese government from 1979 to 1986 required married couples to limit themselves to one child. The age of legal marriage was raised, to 27 for men and 25 for women in urban areas. Free birth control and abortions are available.

Couples who pledge to have only one child receive incentives, such as monthly payments and increased food rations, free health care and schooling, and preferences for housing and jobs. If they have a second child, their salaries and medical benefits are cut back, and they must repay past benefits.

The one-child policy is very unpopular, particularly in the countryside, where large families remain the custom. Sons remain highly valued, and couples who have a girl sometimes resort to murder (infanticide) or continue having children despite government policy.

The Evolving American Model

The first European settlers in North America had to cut their ties to relatives in their homeland and cross the Atlantic on their own. In the colonies, families were virtually self-sufficient. They built their own homes and furniture, grew their own food, wove cloth, and made most household products.

As settlers pushed into the American West, the family often had to serve as the sole tie among people, providing cultural, religious, and emotional support.

THE FAMILY

A mother poses with her seven children and a visitor. Black Americans have been sorely tested by economic adversity and social hostility, yet their families, often headed by strong women, endure.

Husbands were legally responsible for wives, who held no personal property, not even their clothing. Women had higher status in the South than the North, in part because women were scarce in the early days of colonization in the South.

Marriages often were arranged for economic reasons. The average age of grooms was 24 or 25 years; for brides, 22 or 23 years. In remote areas or on the frontier, many couples practiced "self-marriage" and simply declared themselves man and wife until a minister or official could formalize their relationship. This established the precedent for today's "common law" marriages.

The exploration and settlement of the West further undermined the father-centered extended family. Children could not know their grandparents if the family had pushed West, and although fathers were in charge, mothers had to be tough and often equal partners.

As cities grew in the 1800s, family structure changed. No longer did father, mother, and children work to grow their food and make their clothes. Instead, more fathers went out of the home

The History of the Family

to earn a living. Children, once an asset for their contribution at home, became a liability in crowded city dwellings. The birthrate fell.

Industrialization and urbanization have tended to transform the large, authoritarian, rural family system into a smaller, more egalitarian, less stable nuclear unit. The major trends leading to the family as we now know it include women's achievement of nearly equal status and economic independence, and the greater availability and acceptance of divorce.

Black Families Blacks first arrived in the colonies in 1619 in what is now the state of Virginia. Taken from their families and native land, sold away from parents, children, and mates, they struggled to adapt to a culture they had not chosen. Men often had to stay in separate quarters from women, so the strongest ties were between mothers and children—a pattern that persisted long after emancipation in 1863.

The migration of southern blacks into northern cities—which began after the Civil War, sped up with World War I, and continued through the 1960s—created further strains on families, including extreme overcrowding and poverty. More than 70% of the 26 million black Americans now live in urban areas. More than a third meet the government's definition for poverty.

Like white American families, black American families are continuing to evolve and change as they adapt to new circumstances and challenges. Their survival in an often racist and hostile social environment may be tied to what sociologists call their close kinship bonds and deep religious values.

Hispanic Families The families of Spanish settlers of Latin America and South America were, like those of Spain, firmly patriarchal. A woman could not make major financial transactions and could not appear in court without her husband's permission. Divorce was forbidden by the Roman Catholic church.

By the middle of the 20th century, different family forms had evolved among Hispanics, determined mainly by social class. In upper-class families, fathers, who usually were business or professional men, continued to dominate. Wives played submissive roles and had lives of relative ease.

In urban lower-class families, fathers were manual workers; mothers also worked to help make ends meet. The concept of "machismo," which ties a man's feelings of self-worth to his abil-

THE FAMILY

ity to father children and to have extramarital relationships, complicated lower-class marriages. Though wives were not as subordinate as in the upper classes, they were often bound by the duties of child bearing. Divorce, though forbidden by the Roman Catholic church, was the unofficial end of some marriages.

When Hispanic families immigrate to the United States, their structure changes, but not entirely. The degree of change depends on how long the family has lived in the U.S., whether they speak English, how educated they are, and whether the wife works. Both men and women tend to follow the principle of male dominance, but to a lesser extent than in their native countries.

• • • •

CHAPTER 3

HEREDITY: THE BIOLOGY OF THE FAMILY

Families share more than a name or address. You may have your grandmother's eyes, your uncle's ears, or your mother's hands. They are part of your genetic legacy—and the elements of this legacy are more than skin deep. The genes that you inherit from your parents influence everything from your physical makeup to your life span. They may also determine less identifiable traits such as musical ability, thought processes, or susceptibility to certain illnesses, though these characteristics are also influenced by your environment and upbringing. The extent to which genes shape our behavior is the subject of increasing study.

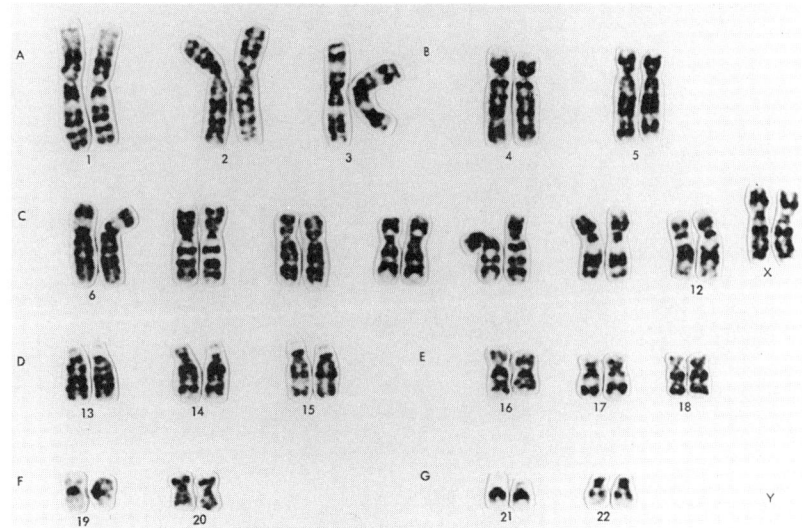

Every normal human cell contains 23 pairs of chromosomes, seen here in a microscopic array; the XX chromosome indicates a female. Each chromosome contains genes, the coded instructions for all biological traits.

What's in Your Genes?

Each human cell contains 23 pairs of chromosomes, rodlike structures that exist within the cell's nucleus. Except for the gametes (egg and sperm), each of the body's billions of cells contains two versions of each chromosome, one from each parent. Arranged along the rodlike chromosomes are the genes, which are composed of *deoxyribonucleic acid,* or DNA. Each gene is the coded instruction for a particular physical characteristic or trait, and each cell possesses two genes for every inherited characteristic. The two genes for a given characteristic may express themselves in the same way or differently. If the actions of the two genes are alike, the person is said to be *homozygous* for that trait. If the actions are different, the person is called *heterozygous.*

One of the heterozygous pair of genes will commonly be dominant over the other, and the trait it determines will appear in the individual. A gene that is not dominant is called recessive. A homozygous pair of genes may be made up of two dominant or two recessive genes.

Brown eyes are a dominant trait. If one parent contributes a gene for brown eyes and the other a gene for blue eyes, the child's eyes will be brown. If both contribute a brown-eyed gene, the eyes will be brown. If both contribute a blue-eyed gene, a recessive trait, the eyes will be blue.

Heredity: The Biology of the Family

How Chromosomes Determine Sex

Scientists have numbered the standard 23 chromosomes in order to differentiate and study them. Chromosomes 1 through 22 in the set from one parent are similar in size, shape, and gene makeup to the set from the other parent. It is the sex-determining chromosomes, pair 23, that are different. In the female, they are both X chromosomes. In the male, there is one X and one Y chromosome. Although different in shape and size, the X and Y chromosomes behave as a pair when sperm and egg cells are produced. Only one chromosome of each pair goes to each egg or sperm.

When the female produces an egg, it gets only one X chromosome. A sperm gets either an X or a Y. When an X-bearing egg combines with an X-bearing sperm, the XX zygote (fertilized egg cell) develops into a female. When an X-bearing egg combines with a Y-bearing sperm, an XY zygote is formed and, because of the Y chromosome, develops into a male.

It was only in 1987 that scientists learned that a single gene rather than several genes on the Y chromosome is responsible for activating the formation of male sex characteristics. The en-

A mother, father, and their twelve daughters. As researchers learn more about heredity, they may discover whether families such as this one are a matter of chance or of genetics.

THE FAMILY

tire Y chromosome contains about 70 million base pairs of DNA, and the portion of it considered the "switch" for male-trait formation contains only 140,000 of those pairs, a remarkably small number considering the enormous changes it triggers in the body's development.

Genetic Defects

Traits determined by certain genes may cause physical developments that deviate from the norm. If the deviation is slight, such as color blindness (a male-linked abnormality), the person will be able to survive in spite of the abnormality, though he may experience minor inconveniences such as difficulty in matching pairs of socks; more severe color blindness may disqualify him from military service or certain lines of work.

A more serious though still not lethal abnormality could result from a flaw in a person's sex-determining gene. Molecular biologists discovered the sex-determining gene in part by examining

This pair of identical twins had cystic fibrosis, a fatal genetic defect inherited from a parent. Genetic disorders account for a high percentage of miscarriages, birth defects, and illnesses.

Heredity: The Biology of the Family

rare cases in which a person with the Y chromosome had in fact developed as a female, or a person with two X chromosomes had developed as a male. In these cases, the tiny genetic "switch" on the Y chromosome had either failed to operate or had drifted to the X chromosome. Victims of this rare aberration will survive, though they will have various physical problems as they reach sexual maturity.

Some genetic defects are more serious still, such as muscular dystrophy, which some people survive if given good care; many other victims, however, die by early adulthood. And genetically linked defects can even prevent an embryo from developing in the womb, causing it to die before birth.

Dominant genes that threaten survival are easily spotted in the parent, but of far greater concern are recessive genes that may be lethal. They will not be noticed unless both partners contribute the same recessive gene. Theoretically, a recessive trait can be hidden for generations, and as long as the trait is masked by a dominant gene, it is not a threat.

These genes may become visible when close relatives produce offspring; because they have similar hereditary backgrounds, both are likely to carry the same recessive genes. The biological problem of producing children who might inherit a trait leaving them disabled or vulnerable to lethal disease is one reason for the common ban on marriages between siblings or first cousins.

Medical scientists do not know why flaws sometimes occur in a set of genetic instructions, but such mistakes are not uncommon. Major genetic disorders may be responsible for a third to a half of all miscarriages, and 2 to 4% of newborns have some genetic abnormality. There is probably a genetic component in almost all diseases; genetic errors are the known cause of thousands of maladies.

The most common genetic problems in American families are as follows:

- Cystic fibrosis: A disabling abnormality of the sweat and mucus glands, marked especially by faulty digestion, difficulty in breathing, and excessive loss of salt in the sweat. Four to 5% of Americans carry the defective gene for this problem but are asymptomatic (showing no symptoms). About one-tenth of 1% of the American population, or one in a thousand, are symptomatic (showing symptoms), and most are whites.

37

THE FAMILY

- Sickle-cell anemia: One of every 400 black children born in the United States each year has this blood disorder in which hemoglobin (the oxygen-carrying protein of red blood cells) is abnormal and fails to carry adequate oxygen to the body's vital organs, causing a number of symptoms. When the abnormal, sickle-shaped cells logjam and block certain blood vessels, they may cut off the oxygen flow and lead to extreme pain, crippling, and death.

- Phenylketonuria (PKU): A recessive genetic disease in which the liver enzyme needed by the body for the metabolism of the amino acid phenylalanine is absent. The affected child may show a progressive mental decline beginning at about age four months. If both parents are carriers, there is a one-in-four chance their child will develop the disease. In most states, the law requires PKU testing of newborns. If the disorder is detected, the infant is placed on an immediate, long-term therapeutic diet to reduce the effects. If untreated, the victim becomes severely mentally retarded.

- Tay-Sachs disease: An enzyme deficiency occurring almost exclusively among young children of Eastern European Jewish ancestry. The infant appears normal in its first six to nine months; then its development rate slows down. The child loses mobility, and speech is im-

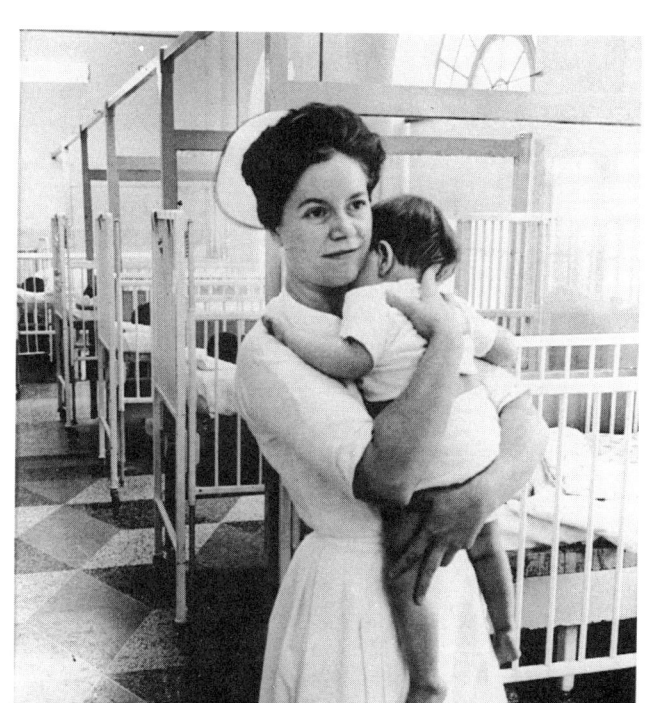

An infant victim of Tay-Sachs disease, an inherited, fatal disease found in some people whose ancestors come from among the Jewish population near the Polish-Russian border.

Heredity: The Biology of the Family

Down's syndrome, in which the child is born with 47 instead of 46 chromosomes in each cell, is an example of a chromosome abnormality. The victims suffer some physical as well as mental retardation.

paired. Death usually occurs before the fifth birthday. One in every 30 people of Eastern European Jewish descent is a carrier. Because the trait is recessive (like PKU), both parents must carry it to affect their child. If both are carriers, the chances of their child being affected are one in four. Carriers can be identified by a blood test.

- Chromosome abnormalities: Fertilized eggs with an abnormal number of chromosomes, or with detectably large parts of chromosomes missing or extra, usually develop abnormally and do not survive pregnancy. If a child is born, it may be abnormal, as in the case of Down's syndrome, in which the infant possesses 47 chromosomes; it is born with deformities of the face, tongue, eyelids, and other parts of the body and is physically and mentally retarded. The chance of a woman delivering a Down's infant increases with her age. At age 25, the chances are 1 in 1,200; at 35, 1 in 365; at 40, 1 in 100.

THE FAMILY

You can also inherit a predisposition or vulnerability to many other disorders, including heart disease, manic depression, and alcoholism. Heredity may play a role in strokes, breast and colon cancer, and schizophrenia, a severe mental disorder whose victims suffer various emotional and personality problems.

Diagnosing Genetic Disorders Scientists are using genetic marker tests to search for a targeted sequence of genes that are inherited in families with a genetic defect. The marker is not the faulty gene itself but appears with it. Because of this technique,

GENETIC DISEASES

Some Diseases that Can Be Detected

Disease	Symptoms	Incidence*
Cystic fibrosis	Liver, lung, pancreas disease	1 in 2,000 Caucasians
Muscular dystrophy	Wasting muscle disease	1 in 5,000 males
Fragile X syndrome	Mental retardation	1 in 1,000 males (primarily)
Hemophilia	Bleeding disorder	1 in 5,000 males
Huntington's chorea	Fatal brain disease	1 in 20,000
Polycystic kidney disease	Kidney failure	1 in 1,000
Tay-Sachs disease	Fatal enzyme deficiency	1 in 3,600 Ashkenazi Jews
Sickle cell anemia	Affects hemoglobin	1 in 400 U.S. blacks (primarily)
Beta thalassemia	Affects spleen and blood	Varies with race and region

Some Diseases with Tests in the Works

Disease	Symptoms	Number of cases†
Alzheimer's disease	Senile dementia	4 million
Manic depression	Severe mood swings	2 million
Heart disease	Heart attacks, hypertension	62 million

Some Diseases With Suspected Genetic Links

Disease	Suspected link	Number of cases†
Stroke	Family history	1.9 million living cases
Breast or colon cancer	Suspected dominant gene	Over 115,000 annual cases each
Schizophrenia	Family history	2 to 3 million living cases

*Estimated cases per number of live births
†Estimates are for U.S. population
Sources: National Academy of Sciences, National Institutes of Health, President's Commission for the Study of Ethical Problems in Medicine, *Western Journal of Medicine*.

which is 95% accurate, scientists have been able to detect signs of an ever-growing list of disorders, including Huntington's, a degenerative brain disease that strikes around age 40. The folk-singer Woody Guthrie died from Huntington's disease.

Many genetic diseases can now be diagnosed before birth. In *amniocentesis*, the most common procedure, a small amount of the amniotic fluid surrounding the fetus is withdrawn into a syringe by a doctor. The fluid contains cells shed by the fetus, which are then grown for two to three weeks in tissue culture, a lab process that replicates the body's organic action. Amniocentesis cannot be performed until a woman is 14 to 16 weeks pregnant. The major risk, that of miscarriage, is less than 1%.

Amniocentesis is usually recommended only if the mother is over 35, has already had a child with a genetic defect, or is known to be a carrier of a detectable genetic disorder.

Chorionic villi sampling is a newer method for testing for genetic defects. The technique is being tested in only a few institutions, and there are still important questions about its safety and reliability, but it provides a very early warning. At 8 to 10 weeks of pregnancy, an obstetrician, guided by ultrasound waves, suctions out a small sample of the chorionic villi, the tissue surrounding the fetus. Laboratory analysis produces the same genetic information as amniocentesis within 24 hours.

If a serious defect is detected in the sampling, the choice to have an abortion can still be made in the first trimester of pregnancy, when it is a comparatively safe operation. Abortion after amniocentesis, which is not done until the second trimester, is much riskier.

Genetic Counseling

A genetic counselor is a highly trained professional who can give parents information about risks to their unborn children, based on family medical histories and, in some cases, tests to determine if the parents are carriers of any potentially troublesome genes. But the parents must still make their own decisions.

If test results are normal, parents can gain reassurance that certain problems, like Down's syndrome, will not arise in their child. If the results show an abnormality, the parents must choose whether to terminate the pregnancy. The counselor can help the parents assess the impact the birth defect might have on themselves, their children, and their children's children.

THE FAMILY

There are moral and ethical issues at stake, too, when genetic counseling is undertaken. Will the pregnancy be terminated if the fetus has a major defect? A minor one? If it carries a one-in-four chance of developing a fatal malady? A one-in-two chance? If the defect is major, how painful and difficult will the baby's existence be? How will the family cope with a possibly severely handicapped child and the subsequent stress it creates in the home? More fundamentally, should the genetic counselor have the right to assist the parents in the decision, or should he or she merely provide information?

Genetic counseling bears the ability to shield most parents from having a genetically abnormal baby, and, theoretically, the entire human race could benefit. But is it right to alter the biological makeup of the species just to suit our needs or convenience? These are questions every parent must face.

•   •   •   •

CHAPTER 4

THE FAMILY LIFE CYCLE

Four generations, 1890s

Like individuals, families grow and evolve, passing with time through predictable stages. Each phase of family development brings new challenges, new tasks, and new rewards.

Ideally, young people go through the sometimes painful process of becoming emotionally and economically independent before forming a new family unit. They establish adult identities, develop close and supportive friendships with their peers, and find a way to earn a living. If young adults marry only to escape their first family, however, they face a greater challenge, for they must find themselves as individuals before they can define themselves as a couple.

Commitment and Marriage

Throughout history marriage has symbolized the birth of a new family. Sometimes couples do not formalize their commitment to each other. An estimated 2 million American men and women live together without a legal marital agreement.

With or without marriage, two people who decide to share their lives have considerable adjusting to do. Each brings to the relationship a set of expectations and rules acquired in their families of origin. Inevitably, they have to negotiate and compromise, working out such personal issues as when and how to sleep, eat, make love, fight, and make up. They must decide how to celebrate holidays, plan vacations, spend money, and do household chores.

As a couple, young people separate even more from their families of origin. One partner's parents become the other's in-laws, and tensions may develop if the in-laws try to remain too involved in their grown child's life.

The transition from the independence of living alone to the constant negotiations of living together can be extremely stressful. The majority of wives now work, and two-career couples face extra stresses: Both may come home tired and irritable; both may have to travel or work weekends. And they must deal with difficult issues: What if one earns more money? What if one is transferred?

A few rare couples resolve those dilemmas by working in different cities and spending weekends together. Others try to alternate career priorities. However imperfect these arrangements may be, they can work if both partners are willing to compromise for the sake of their relationship.

Becoming Parents

The birth of the first child changes the rules for every couple. In fact, having a baby may demand more adjustments than getting married did. In studies of new parents, sociologists Carolyn and Philip Cowan of the University of California found that parents tend to assume far more traditional roles, with the mother taking on most of the care-giving responsibilities and the father focusing on his duty as breadwinner.

Marital satisfaction can decline after the baby arrives, and the separation and divorce rates climb at that point. But if the re-

The Family Life Cycle

lationship's bonds were strong before the baby's arrival, the couple usually endures. Shaky marriages are the ones most likely to shatter.

An infant may fascinate and thrill new parents, but the adjustment to a baby-centered life can cause resentment. The husband who feels that his wife is more concerned with the baby than with him often feels jealous, which in turn makes him feel guilty. The mother, still recovering from an enormous physical and psychological upheaval, may feel overwhelmed by the new responsibilities.

When they become parents, both husband and wife "move up" a generation and take on a new range of developmental tasks: sharing parental responsibility, developing patience, tolerating the restrictions on their independence and free time. They must learn, however reluctantly, to put the baby before their individual wishes and needs.

Accepting the New Personality An entire household may focus on the immense, immediate needs of a newborn, but soon parents face another task: dealing not just with a mouth to be fed and a body to be kept clean and warm but with a unique person.

Scouting is one of several early childhood activities that foster autonomy and the beginnings of healthy separation from parents.

THE FAMILY

Loving and productive experiences shared between parent and child can be as important in communicating values as are rules and regulations.

No child is born into the world as a blank slate. Babies are born with likes and dislikes, responses, reactions, and characteristic personalities. Recent studies show that the baby may have as much effect on the parents' behavior as they have on the baby's. For example, the baby who makes eye contact with the parents and who smiles is more likely to get their attention than a child who fusses and does not respond to cuddling.

As babies grow into toddlers and preschoolers, parents must set limits on their behavior, establish values of what is right or wrong, and guide by example as well as by words. Some counselors feel that children become failures or successes because of the messages conveyed by their parents early in life.

Introducing the Child to the World As children grow, parents must make the first arrangements for them to enter the institutions of society: school, church, scouts, sports groups. The parents must prepare the children so they know what to expect, assure the child's safety, and establish good working relationships with teachers, coaches, and counselors.

At home, school-age children can take on more responsibility in the family: making beds, setting the table, caring for pets. However, with each year, the tug between independence and dependence becomes harder. Children are drawn into the world, and their parents are torn between clinging to them or pushing them out of the nest. It is not enough to set rules; parents must advise a child on how to make decisions within the rules.

The transition from childhood to adulthood is, for parents and children, the best and worst of times. Children becoming teenagers develop more responsibility, more sense of self, more independence. Simultaneously, they may rebel, challenging and testing their parents. A child's emerging sexuality may be difficult for the parents to acknowledge and accept.

Experiments in Independence Teenagers have their own value systems, which may clash with those of their parents. Setting limits—curfews, dating guidelines, weekend trips—may trigger a confrontation rather than be a simple matter of stating policy. Many teenagers have a strong desire to separate from their parents, but they may also feel drawn back to the security of the home.

Adolescence can be the most difficult period for parent and child alike. As children grow into adolescence, they begin to find it necessary to assert their independence, inevitably causing some degree of tension.

THE FAMILY

Adolescence is a time of tremendous growth and change. During this time young people begin to explore their social and sexual identities.

Young people in their late teens and early twenties hover between dependence and independence, immaturity and maturity. For many, college provides a place to take charge of their daily lives without taking on the burden of supporting themselves.

Increasingly, young people are not moving straight from college into an independent life. In a 1983 survey, 59% of 18- to 24-year-olds were living with their parents, compared to 48.2% in 1970. However, almost all young adults eventually face the world on their own, and their parents must come to accept them as independent, self-sufficient adults.

Middle Age

As life spans have lengthened, the later life stages have become longer. Many couples who have spent perhaps 3 years together before having children will live childlessly for 15 or 20 years.

Aging families might consist of a couple married for many years or of a single spouse, left alone because of death or divorce. The survivor may remarry, creating an extended family with many new members.

The Family Life Cycle

Husbands and wives alone in their marriages must once more redefine themselves as partners, not parents. Their other tasks include providing for their own comfort and needs and setting aside resources for the future. They also may look increasingly beyond the home, establishing new friendships or rekindling old ones and cultivating new interests.

Another responsibility they face is caring for their own parents, who may have become more dependent or require attention because of illness and age. When the family's eldest members die, their children must cope with grief and the stark reality that they now are the "older" generation.

Aging

One of the joys for aging couples is becoming grandparents. Grandchildren offer a second chance to enjoy parenthood with far fewer anxieties and responsibilities. Grandparents have the luxury of time and the wisdom to be patient. These are the gifts they offer each grandchild who enters the family.

In the past, aging parents tended to live with their children's families. That custom has changed dramatically—not just because children live farther away or may be separated or divorced but because all parties seem to prefer their independence.

Yet the custom has been modified and updated for some families. With more mothers now holding jobs, and with the rising expense of babysitters and day-care facilities, grandparents are again called upon to mind the children. It is a service that most provide willingly, though there is a slight danger if the parents take the grandparents' assistance for granted. Many retired people are busy with their own lives and homes and cannot be as devoted to their grandchildren as they were in the days when extended families lived together.

A sign of the comparative vigor of older Americans today is that nearly half of those over 65 own their own homes. Fewer than 5%—1.3 million Americans—live in nursing homes. The percentage in nursing homes rises with age, from barely 1% of men and women between 65 and 74 to 22% of those 85 or older.

More than half of Americans over 65 are married or live together in 2-person households. But for women, who generally outlive their husbands, the likelihood of their living alone rises with time. Of those between 65 and 74, 27% live alone, as do 31% of those between 75 and 84 and 40% of those over 85.

THE FAMILY

As they enter their late seventies or their eighties, parents may have to relinquish power and status, depend more on their children, and come to terms with illnesses and physical limitations. With the death of one partner, the other may require greater care from the children.

In other cultures, family elders were venerated for their wisdom. Our society is less mindful of the special contributions aging parents can make. Yet, as they grow old and long after they die, our parents and our parents' parents live on in our hearts, part of us and our families forever.

• • • •

CHAPTER 5

FAMILY PLANNING

Two sides of the abortion debate

The ability to become parents by choice, not chance, has had a profound impact on the size and structure of modern families. With the development of reasonably safe and effective methods of birth control, couples have many more options than they did even 20 years ago or than couples do in the less-developed nations of the world. One result of these greater choices is that many couples, especially educated ones, are not having children until later in their marriage.

THE FAMILY

Freed from worry about unwanted pregnancies, both partners can pursue careers and work toward economic independence. They can establish more-equal roles in their marriages. With less of their income spent on child raising, they have more financial and personal options.

One-third of all married couples say they plan not to have children. By contrast, a generation ago only one-fifth of married couples were childless, and for many of those couples that situation was involuntary.

There are good and bad, mature and immature, logical and illogical reasons for having a child. Some people want to prove they are no longer children themselves. Some want someone to love and be loved by. Some hope children will hold together a crumbling relationship. Some want only to extend their love for each other to another person. Some see the child egotistically—as a replication of themselves.

Would-be parents should discuss their reasons for wanting or not wanting children to make sure they are being realistic in their expectations. They should decide whether they are willing to make the necessary accommodations and take on the responsibilities entailed. Children are expensive; they often lower the couple's standard of living. The estimated cost of caring for one child from birth until college graduation is $135,000.

Couples who decide not to have a child, though still in the minority, will be a growing portion of the population in the 21st century. And, according to marital therapists, many of them are as likely, if not more so, to be as contented as the couples with children.

BIRTH CONTROL

Deciding whether to use birth control is a decision that has to be made simultaneously with the decision to be sexually active.

Why do some people—particularly the young—avoid contraceptives? Ignorance is often the reason. Some teenage girls engaging in intercourse without contraceptive protection think that they cannot become pregnant if they simply do not want to or do not have an orgasm or have intercourse in certain positions, such as standing up. Other teenagers understand the various methods of birth control, but they often fail to use them properly

Family Planning

The estimated cost of raising one child from crib through college is over $135,000. For many middle-class families the cost of a college education is becoming prohibitive.

or at all, particularly the first time they have sexual intercourse. Some feel that taking precautions to prevent pregnancy implies sexual availability.

There are other reasons for not practicing contraception. Some people do not have access to good medical services and advice, especially if they are poor or if the counselor is legally restricted (as in some states) from giving advice to a minor without the parents' consent. And there are millions of people, most notably Roman Catholics, whose religious beliefs forbid them from practicing birth control.

Only one form of birth control is completely safe and effective: abstaining from sexual intercourse. Kissing, hugging, and touching are "safe" forms of sexual contact.

The Birth Control Pill

Oral contraceptives are the most common birth-control method for unmarried women and those under 30. More than 60 million women, including 9 million in the United States, take the pill. Three types are available: a combination pill, a multiphasic pill, and a mini pill. They each contain one or more natural or synthetic sex hormone. Estrogen and progesterone are hormones that play an important role in regulating a woman's menstrual cycle and the physical changes she undergoes during puberty. The balance of hormones in a woman's system controls her menstrual cycle and monthly ovulation, or release of an egg cell, during which time a woman is fertile. Essentially, birth control pills work by preventing ovulation.

When the pill was first introduced in the mid-1950s, it contained much higher levels of the hormone estrogen than were necessary. Consequently, many undesirable side effects were noted, including wild mood swings, increased risk of breast cancer and cancer of the female reproductive organs, hormonal imbalances, menstrual difficulties, and a higher mortality rate among users. Although today's oral contraceptives contain much lower doses of estrogen and other hormones, their use still involves risks and side effects, especially among women who smoke and/or who are over the age of 35.

The combination pill contains two hormones, synthetic estrogen and progestin, a progesteronelike substance. Different brands of the combination pills contain varying balances of these hormones. A woman's doctor can help her decide which one is best suited for her. Women may experience different side effects with different pills. These side effects may include tender breasts, nausea or vomiting, and gain or loss of weight. More serious side effects such as blood clots or high blood pressure may also occur, although more infrequently. These risks increase as a woman gets older or if she smokes.

The multiphasic pill provides different levels of estrogen and progesterone at different times of the month to simulate the normal hormonal fluctuations of the natural menstrual cycle. These pills contain a lower total dose of hormones than the combination pill, which often reduces the side effects. The combination pill and the multiphasic pill are 99% effective, meaning that over the course of a year only one woman in a hundred will become pregnant while taking these pills.

The mini pill contains a small amount of progestin and no estrogen. Unlike the women who take combination pills, those using mini pills probably do ovulate at least occasionally. The mini pills, however, make the mucus in the cervix so thick that sperm cannot enter the uterus. The mini pill is 97 to 98% effective.

The "morning-after" pill is the name commonly used to refer to several types of medication sometimes prescribed after a woman has had unprotected intercourse, if a woman fears there may have been a failure with the contraceptive method she was using (e.g., a condom ripped during intercourse), or in an emergency situation such as rape. A woman must take this pill within hours after intercourse for it to be effective. The morning-after pill works by affecting the uterine lining in a way that prevents implantation of a fertilized egg. The large doses of estrogen and progestin contained in some of these pills may have undesirable side effects. This method should be considered only as a backup in emergency situations. In fact, many doctors will not even prescribe a morning-after pill.

Barrier Contraceptives

As their name implies, barrier contraceptive forms of birth control block the meeting of egg and sperm by means of a physical barrier: a diaphragm, a cervical cap, a contraceptive sponge, or a condom. Barrier contraceptives have become increasingly popular because they can do more than prevent conception; when used with certain spermicides (sperm-killing chemicals), they can help protect users from sexually transmitted diseases, including syphilis and chlamydia. Latex condoms, when used in combination with spermicides containing at least 5% nonoxynol-9 (a chemical ingredient of many spermicides that has been shown to kill some microorganisms), may help prevent the spread of acquired immune deficiency syndrome (AIDS).

A condom is a sheath used to cover the erect penis and catch semen. Condoms are most effective when used in conjunction with a sperm-killing foam, jelly, or film. Although the theoretical effectiveness rate for condoms alone is 90 to 97%, and 99% when used with a spermicide, the actual rate for both is only 80 to 85%. A condom can tear during the manufacturing process or while in use. Careless removal is also a problem. But the main reason that condoms have a low effectiveness rate is that some couples do not use them every time they have intercourse.

A diaphragm is a bowllike rubber cup with a spring rim, in sizes ranging from two to four inches in diameter. Used with a spermicide (available at pharmacies without a prescription) and properly fitted by a physician, a diaphragm acts as a mechanical barrier and a container for a chemical barrier, preventing sperm from entering the uterus. The diaphragm is inserted just prior to intercourse and must remain in place for at least eight hours afterward. If the diaphragm is put in long before intercourse is to take place or if intercourse is to be repeated, additional spermicide must be inserted with an applicator. A diaphragm alone is not effective—its main function is to serve as a container for a sperm-killing foam or jelly. When used properly, with a spermicide, the effectiveness rate for the diaphragm is 98%. When misused or used only sporadically, however, the effectiveness rate drops to about 80%.

Like the diaphragm, the cervical cap acts as a mechanical barrier blocking the path of sperm to the uterus. The rubber or plastic cap, which resembles a large thimble, fits snugly around the cervix. Smaller and thicker than a diaphragm, it is believed to be comparable in effectiveness and can be left in place for up to three days with no additional application of spermicide. The cap, which was approved by the Food and Drug Administration (FDA) for general sale in early 1988, is becoming more widely available. Some of the problems that have been noted concerning use of the cervical cap are the limited number of sizes it comes

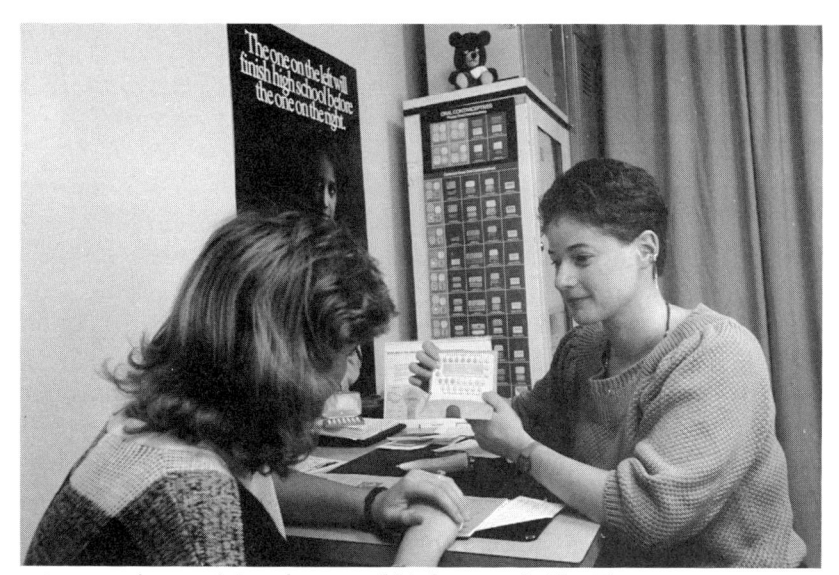

A counselor explains the use of birth-control pills. The teen pregnancy rate is soaring, because many teenagers have not received information about birth control and many more who have do not bother to use it.

in, possible dislodging during intercourse, and the possibility of causing a vaginal discharge if left in place too long.

A contraceptive sponge is a soft, disposable, polyurethane sponge, about two inches in diameter, saturated with the spermicide nonoxynol-9. It is available at pharmacies without a prescription. A woman moistens the sponge, compresses it, and inserts it by hand—a process that is not much more difficult than inserting a tampon. She can put it in place up to 24 hours before intercourse and must leave it in place for 6 hours after intercourse. She removes it by pulling on an attached nylon loop. It cannot be reused. The sponge works in three ways. It acts as a physical barrier to the cervix; the built-in spermicide inactivates the sperm; and the porous sponge absorbs the semen. Though conclusive research has yet to be amassed concerning the side effects of sponge use, some researchers believe that leaving the sponge in place for long periods of time can increase the risk of toxic shock syndrome (TSS), a potentially deadly infection. Although theoretical effectiveness is believed to be in the 90% range, the actual rate of effectiveness in a preliminary study was only 83%.

Spermicides

Modern vaginal spermicides are chemical foams, creams, jellies, vaginal suppositories, and gels. Although some creams and jellies are made for use with a diaphragm, others can be used alone. Those containing nonoxynol-9 also kill organisms that cause some sexually transmitted diseases. Spermicides are introduced into the vaginal area immediately prior to intercourse and must be readministered if intercourse is repeated. Spermicides by themselves are not very effective. Foam has a theoretical effectiveness rate of 95% to 97%, but an actual effectiveness rate of 85% or below. The actual effectiveness rate of suppositories is even lower. Furthermore, not all suppositories are contraceptive, so a woman should read the label very carefully before buying them. When used in combination with one of the barrier contraceptive methods (diaphragms or condoms, for example), the effectiveness rate is much higher.

Vaginal contraceptive film (VCF) is available from pharmacies without a prescription. It is a 2" x 2" thin film square laced with spermicide. Once inserted into the vagina, it dissolves into a gel.

A woman inserts the film by folding it and guiding it in with a finger so it covers the cervix. VCF can be inserted from an hour and a half to five minutes before intercourse. It is effective for up to two hours and dissolves inside the woman's vagina. VCF is comparable in effectiveness to the sponge.

Several adverse side effects have been noted with the use of spermicides. Among these are allergic reactions to the chemicals used in spermicides and irritation, including burning and itching, of both the penis and vagina.

Intrauterine Device

The intrauterine device (IUD) is a device inserted by a physician into the uterus through the cervix. It prevents pregnancy by interfering with the implantation of the fertilized egg in the wall of the uterus. Once a widely used form of birth control, the IUD has become less common and more controversial. IUD use has been linked with increased incidence of pelvic inflammatory disease (PID) and may have such serious side effects as sterility, ectopic (outside the uterus) pregnancy, or perforation of the cervix or uterus. Because of these problems only one brand, the Progestasert, remains on the market. The Progestasert is a small, T-shaped, molded plastic device containing progesterone, a hormone that is slowly released over the course of a year. After a year, the device must be replaced. The effectiveness rate for the IUD is 94 to 99%.

The Rhythm Method

The rhythm method is a natural, nonchemical form of contraception. This method requires the abstinence from intercourse during the fertile time of the menstrual cycle, that is, during the days preceding and just following ovulation. The rhythm method requires careful timing to avoid the possible meeting of a ripe egg and active sperm in the woman's fallopian tubes. It is the only type of contraception permitted and endorsed by the Roman Catholic church.

There are four ways commonly used to detect the woman's fertile period, including the calendar method, body temperature, examination of cervical mucus, and a method called the sympto-thermal method. The calendar method involves careful record keeping and calculation of the time a woman is most fertile. This is not as accurate in younger women who do not yet have completely regular cycles. The temperature method involves the daily use of a special type of thermometer and accurate record keeping. To use the cervical mucus method, a woman must daily observe and record her vaginal secretions. The symptothermal method involves observation of the changes in the cervix as well as in the temperature and mucus.

The effectiveness of these methods greatly depends on correct use. The calendar method is 53 to 86% effective. The temperature method is 80 to 99% effective. The mucus method is 75 to 90% effective. The symptothermal method is 78-99% effective. When two or more of the methods are used together, a more complete and accurate effect is often achieved. For best results with the rhythm method, both the woman and her partner must be willing to consistently abstain from intercourse during part of each month.

Sterilization

Sterilization (surgery that eliminates a person's reproductive capability) is the most popular birth-control method among married couples in the United States, according to the National Center for Health Statistics. About 22% of women who at one time used contraception have had tubal ligations or occlusions (tying or blocking the fallopian tubes) or hysterectomies (removal of the uterus), and 11% of men have had a vasectomy (the surgical division of the duct in the scrotum that carries sperm). Although sterilization procedures can sometimes be reversed, the operation should be considered permanent, and both partners should be sure that they do not want more children (or any children at all, as the case may be). Sterilization is undertaken most often by people who have a family and do not wish to produce any more children, though the procedure is legal for any adult.

Abortion

Abortion is the termination of a pregnancy. More than a million and a half abortions are performed in the United States every year; 30% involve teenagers. Women aged 18 and 19 have the highest abortion rate. Ninety-one percent of the abortions done in the United States are performed during the first trimester (up to 13 weeks after a woman's last menstrual period); 51% are done within 8 weeks; and 40% within 12 weeks.

THE FAMILY

The decision to have an abortion is not a simple one. The reasons women give include not having intended to become pregnant, not having the money or desire to raise a child at that time, and not having a supportive companion. Some women intend to have a baby but develop medical complications with the pregnancy or decide to terminate the pregnancy after genetic tests identify the presence of a birth defect (see Chapter 3 for a discussion of counseling and birth defects).

During the first trimester, abortion is a relatively simple medical procedure. The earlier in the pregnancy the abortion is performed, the safer it is. Ninety-seven percent of the women who

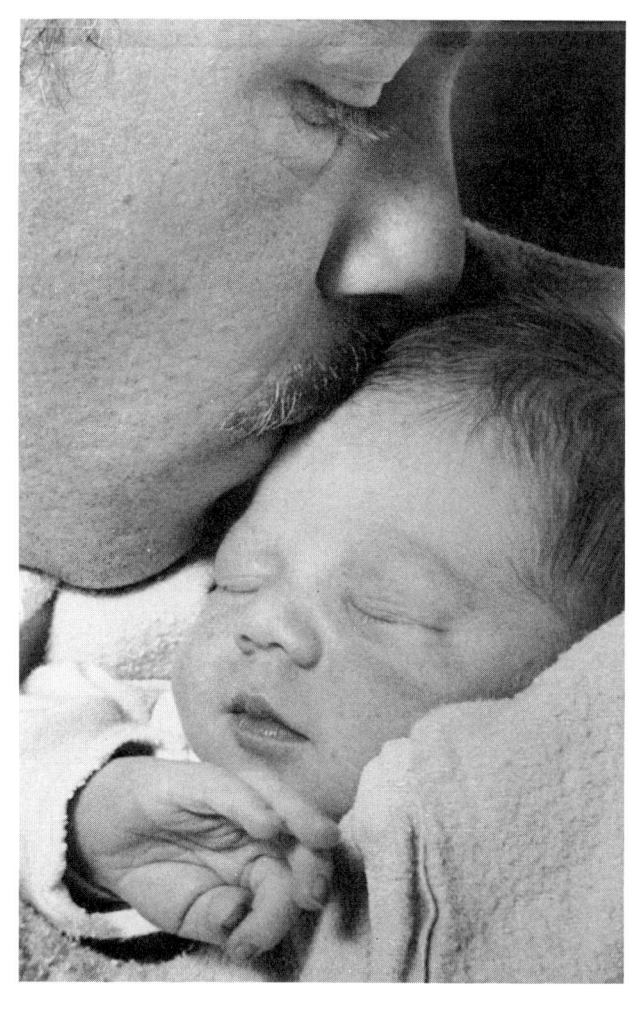

Several ways to bear children through the help of modern medical technology have given hope to infertile or subfertile couples. This newborn boy was implanted as a fertilized embryo into his mother's uterus.

undergo first trimester abortions have no complications. In the second trimester, the chance of complications increases. Sadly, almost half of all second trimester abortions are obtained by teenage girls.

Like the decision whether or not to have sex and the decision about what type of birth control to use, the decision whether or not to have an abortion ideally should be a joint one made by a woman and her partner. These are difficult decisions but ones that must be made. They can be made more easily if a woman has the necessary information and emotional support. Information can be obtained by contacting the agencies listed in the appendix in the back of this book. Discussing the options with her boyfriend or husband, parents, and a member of the clergy may help a woman to arrive at the decision best suited to her unique situation.

There are options other than abortion open to a woman who finds herself with an unplanned pregnancy. She may decide to carry the baby to term and then give it up for adoption. She may decide to have the baby and raise it with or without the assistance of the father. In making this decision, a woman should consider her financial situation, her insurance coverage, her employer's maternity policy, her desire or lack of desire to raise a child, the availability of people who will assist with child care (grandparents, for instance), and her religious and ethical beliefs. There are agencies that she can contact (see appendix) to obtain information on adoption and prenatal care.

INFERTILITY: INVOLUNTARY BIRTH CONTROL

Twenty percent of the couples who marry this year will not be able to conceive a child; an additional 10% of married couples will not be able to have more children. In women, the most common causes of subfertility (less than normal fertility, such as in a woman whose ovaries produce fewer eggs) or of infertility are abnormal menstrual patterns, suppression of ovulation, and blocked fallopian tubes, a primary cause of which is infection. Male infertility can be a consequence of either the quantity or the quality of sperm. Medical treatments can help about 70% of previously infertile couples conceive.

THE FAMILY

New Ways of Making Babies

Increasingly, families who cannot conceive are turning to new techniques that are redefining what it means to be a mother and father:

- Artificial insemination: Sperm is placed into a woman's cervix during the three or four days surrounding ovulation. It is usually inserted with a syringe through a tube. The sperm may come either from the woman's partner or from a donor. This procedure is done in cases in which the woman's partner has a low sperm count, if his sperm carries genetic defects, if for physical or psychological reasons he is unable to ejaculate during intercourse, or if he is totally infertile.

- *In vitro* fertilization: A woman's egg is combined with sperm in a laboratory dish. A fertilized egg cell is then returned to the woman's body for a normal pregnancy and birth. The first test-tube baby, Louise Brown, was born on July 25, 1978, in England. Since then test-tube babies have become more common.

- Gamete intra-fallopian transfer (GIFT): This alternative to in vitro fertilization involves the surgical placement of sperm and eggs into the fallopian tubes to imitate the way a normally fertilized egg would begin its development. The operation is more difficult than in vitro fertilization but less expensive and less time consuming. It is usually performed on women whose tubes are blocked; eggs and sperm are inserted below the point of blockage.

- Embryo transfer: The sperm of the husband of an infertile woman is used to fertilize another woman's egg in the laboratory. The fertilized egg is transferred to the uterus of the man's wife, who carries and delivers the developing embryo.

- Surrogacy: Surrogate mothers are women who are artificially inseminated by the sperm of an infertile woman's husband and who carry the baby to term, sometimes for a fee. After delivery, the surrogate mother turns the baby over to the couple, and may have some visiting rights if their contract so stipulates. There have been some much-publicized cases involving surrogate motherhood, and it will be many years before legal opinion

Family Planning

William and Elizabeth Stern in 1987, after being awarded custody of Baby M. The Sterns had contracted with a surrogate mother, Mary Beth Whitehead, who later sued them to regain custody of the child.

catches up with the medical technology—some states allow it, some have barred it, others have yet to rule.

- Host Uterus: This approach combines sperm and the egg in a laboratory. The fertilized egg is implanted in a second woman who agrees to bear the child, usually for a fee.
- Fertility drugs: There are several drugs used to increase female fertility. Some work by sparking ovulation; some stimulate production of estrogen and progesterone, which prepares the uterus to receive a fertilized egg; others stimulate the pituitary gland to produce the hormones that in turn stimulate estrogen and progesterone production. One of the problems encountered by women who take these drugs is an increase in the number of multiple births (such as twins or triplets).

THE FAMILY

    Whatever the choice a couple makes concerning birth control and family planning, the most important thing is that they discuss all options together. It is two people who begin a family, and it is two people who must agree on how it will be done. In the unfortunate case of a childless couple, their options may have legal or moral ramifications or may have to involve a third person. In any event, the understanding, caring, and love that come out of family-planning discussions can only make the marriage stronger.

•   •   •   •

CHAPTER 6

ALL IN THE FAMILY: FAMILY DYNAMICS

"Happy families are all alike," the novelist Leo Tolstoy wrote in *Anna Karenina*; "every unhappy family is unhappy in its own way." Yet even in happy families, there are tremendous differences, depending on their size, number of children, and the ways in which family members relate to and communicate with each other.

Though there is no such thing as a "perfect" family, some families work together more effectively than others. When family relations and communications break down, professional counselors can help families pick up the pieces and create healthier, happier ways of living together.

THE FAMILY

One and Only

The one-child family is a trend throughout the world. It is government policy in China, and elsewhere it is becoming the family size of choice. In the United States, 13 million children are only children, whereas 20 years ago there were only two-thirds that many. More couples are opting for only one child because of marriage at a later age, the demands of two careers, infertility, and economic pressures. The parents of 35% of only children are divorced, a somewhat lower percentage than for multichild families.

Recent research shows that one-child families are much like two-child families, and "onlies" are as happy and self-reliant as their peers—in childhood and adulthood. Yet only children must contend with some disadvantages, including loneliness, the lack of siblings to teach them the basics of give-and-take, and parental expectations that may be excessively high.

On the plus side, only children get more attention from parents and encounter less tension and fighting in their homes. The economic advantage can be sizable, too, especially compared to a family in which the same income might have to feed three or four more mouths.

Only children consistently score higher on intelligence tests, do better at school, and become higher achievers as adults. This gap may be a result of the only child's greater contact with adult logic and vocabulary from an early age, or possibly the factor of the parents' high expectations.

Siblings

Brothers and sisters teach each other basic lessons in loving and living with other people. The arrival of a sibling changes the world of the first child, who once claimed the parents' attention and love as his or hers exclusively. Like it or not, firstborns must learn to share. In return for what they give up, they gain companions, confidants, and allies against the adult world.

In *The Sibling Bond*, psychologists Stephen B. Bank and Michael D. Kahn describe the special tie between brothers and sisters as "a connection between the two selves, at both the intimate and the public level. . . . the 'fitting' together of two peoples' identities." As they note, this bond may be warm and positive, but it also can be negative.

Sisters and brothers may at times compete with each other for their parents' love and attention. But they also learn from one another how to get along in the world.

Birth Order The way brothers and sisters relate to each other depends to a certain extent on their birth order. Some firstborns differ from their siblings in that they may tend to act more like adults: to set higher standards for themselves, to be well organized, conscientious, serious, and reliable.

Middleborns may get less attention than the firstborn or the youngest, a position that can lead them to become the family mediators, doing everything possible to avoid conflict. They may reach beyond the family to make many friends, to whom they are fiercely loyal.

Lastborns may be more adored and protected by parents and siblings. The consequences of such special treatment may range from dependence to sociability to blooming optimism.

It should be noted, however, that every one of these descriptions can apply to any child in any family. A multiplicity of factors are involved in each child's psychological development, including sex, genetic makeup, and the number of years separating him or her from other siblings. Judgments of how birth order affects a child are hardly a science; instead, they are a favorite topic for amateur psychologists, a group that includes almost everyone.

THE FAMILY

Sibling Rivalry In any family with several children, some sibling rivalry is inevitable as they compete for their parents' attention. One technique parents can use to defuse sibling rivalry is to avoid comparisons. Instead of pointing out that one child is neater or smarter (or less so) than another, parents should describe their children's good or bad behavior on an individual basis: "You did a great job cleaning your room," or "It seems that you did not study for your spelling test."

As Adele Faber and Elaine Mazlish point out in *Siblings Without Rivalry*, the goal for parents and children should be "a world in which brothers and sisters grow up in homes where hurting isn't allowed, where children are taught to express their anger at each other sanely and safely, where each child is valued as an individual, not in relation to the others, where cooperation, rather than competition, is the norm, where no one is trapped in a role, where children have daily experience and guidance in resolving their differences."

Grandparents can add much to a youngster's life—as teachers, playmates, confidants, and as links to an entire family's history.

Grandparents

Grandparents are part of a love story between generations. To them, grandchildren are a vision of the future, and most take enormous pleasure and pride in their children's children.

Among the styles of grandparenting are the following rough categories:

- Formal: Grandparents who provide presents and treats and occasionally babysit.
- Funseeker: Grandparents who are interested in and enjoy playing with their grandchildren and leave discipline to the parents.
- Surrogate: Grandparents who take an active role in bringing up grandchildren, usually when both parents work full-time.
- Reservoir of family wisdom: Grandparents who feel they can show grandchildren what is right and wrong and instill moral values.
- Distant: Grandparents who rarely have any contact with their grandchildren.

There is most likely a little bit of each one of these traits in every grandparent, and circumstances such as distance, age, and need will determine which "style" emerges strongest.

In any case, grandparents can add a special dimension to the lives of young children. They delight them with tales of what their parents were like when they were young. They recognize and appreciate each child's individual strengths. They offer reassurance that someone other than parents can love and take care of them. And without any conscious effort, they teach those at the beginning of life about its end, about how it looks and feels to be older.

Happy Families

There is no one formula for successful families, but researchers have identified certain characteristics of happy families. In a survey of more than 3,000 families of different social and economic status, race, religion, education, and age in their book *Secrets of Strong Families,* authors Nick Stinnett and John DeFrain found six major qualities contributing to a family's strength and contentment:

THE FAMILY

- Commitment: Members of strong families are dedicated to each other's welfare and happiness. Through good times and bad, they give each other steady, lasting emotional support.
- Appreciation: In happy families, parents and children frequently let each other know that they are appreciated. Compliments are given more often than criticism, especially during setbacks.
- Communication: Strong families spend a lot of time talking to each other. Some meet regularly in a "family council" to air gripes and discuss problems. Others casually share information about what they are doing and thinking, often at the dinner table. Happy families do fight, but they work at fighting fair. That means no bullying, dominating, blaming, or controlling others.
- Time together: Strong families do not choose between quality time and quantity of time spent together. They believe that quality and quantity go hand in hand. Each family member may have individual interests, but all come together to participate in activities everyone can enjoy, such as picnicking or going to the beach.
- Spiritual wellness: Whether or not they attend formal religious services, strong families share a belief in a higher power or greater good. This belief gives them a sense of purpose and the strength to cope with life's ups and downs.
- Crises and stress: Happy families are not immune to life's major and minor disasters but are less prone to be overwhelmed by crises. They work at keeping daily hassles in perspective and trying to look for the positives in difficult situations.

Other researchers expand this list to include traits such as respect for each other, mutual trust, flexibility, spontaneity, and a common sense of right and wrong.

Family Therapy When families can no longer fulfill their functions, professional counselors—usually psychologists, psychiatrists, or social workers with special training in family issues—can help them break out of destructive emotional patterns.

The most common reasons for seeking professional help are marital problems, severe sibling rivalry, and enmeshed conflict

The Forgotten Teenage Father

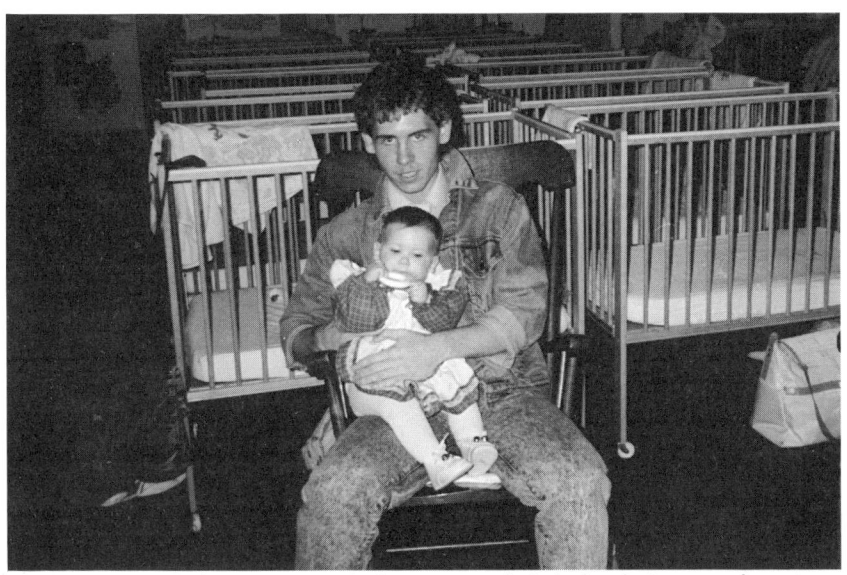

Most teenage fathers want to help support their baby, but many do not know how. At this clinic in Kentucky, young fathers learn about child care.

Teenage fathers are generally viewed as irresponsible and indifferent young men, unconcerned about their children or their children's mothers. Yet their lives, too, are changed by the birth of a child. They get less education and earn lower incomes than men who wait until age 20 to have a child.

Although most do not marry the mothers, they are not all uncaring. In a 2-year pilot program that offered vocational services, counseling, and prenatal and parenting classes to nearly 400 teenage fathers and prospective fathers in 8 U.S. cities, young fathers showed that they were eager to help their partner and child.

Almost 90% maintained a relationship with the mother; 82% had daily contact with the child; 74% contributed to the child's support. Of those who had dropped out of school, 46% returned to school, and 61% of those previously unemployed found jobs. The researchers' conclusion: "A lot of teenage fathers want to love their babies and do the right thing for them, but they don't see how to do what is right."

between parents and children. Often, teenage rebellion against parental authority brings families into counselors' offices for the first time.

Increasingly, drug abuse by one or more family members can lead them to seek therapy. Catastrophic illness, a devastating accident, or death are also among the events that can jolt a once-happy family into a period of turmoil.

Family therapy usually involves every family member at some point. However, the therapist may also choose to see the parents or the children alone or in different combinations. The success of family therapy depends on open communication and the courage to risk exposing the truth. Its goal is to identify and change harmful behavior patterns within the family; to ease the family through rocky times; and to create new, more positive ways of relating.

• • • •

CHAPTER 7

DIVORCE AND SINGLE-PARENT FAMILIES

One of every eight American marriages ends in divorce. And then, for the 1 million children newly caught up in divorces every year, there is further unhappiness: life with one parent or, if both share custody, life in two homes.

In the last two decades, the number of two-parent families has declined, and the number of one-parent families has soared. In the mid-1980s, nearly 26% of American children were living in single-parent homes, double the 1970 rate. Researchers estimate that more than half of the children born in 1987 will spend at least one year living in a single-parent household before they are 18 years old.

THE FAMILY

From "I Do" to "I Don't"

Once, most people married for as long as they both should live; today they are more likely to marry for as long as they both love. When love ends—whatever the reason—the marriage ends as well.

The divorce rate among American couples (and elsewhere in the world too) soared to the highest levels in history in the late 1970s. Since then, it has been inching downward. Divorce has not proven to be the cure for what ails an unhappy relationship. In a 10-year study of 60 divorced American couples, Judith Wallerstein, executive director of the Center for the Family in Transition in Corte Madera, California, found only 19% of the divorced people thought both spouses' lives had improved after their marriages ended.

For women, divorce can have a devastating economic impact. The incomes of women who do not remarry after a divorce fall by an average of 30%. Among black women, the decline is even greater—54%. The majority of women, especially black women, receive no child support, often because the laws requiring the former husband to pay it are difficult to enforce. After divorce,

A man responds to his wife's divorce suit by sawing their house in half. Divorce rates in the industrialized nations seem to be slowing down in the 1980s, after hitting all-time highs in the 1970s.

the percentage of mothers who work outside the home increases from 66 to 90%. Yet the median income for divorced women is 42% lower than that of married couples.

CHILDREN OF DIVORCE

For children, the effects of divorce go far beyond finances. Divorce means the death of the family they have known, and they may mourn its loss longer than either parent does. A child's adjustment to divorce depends partially on his or her age and on the discord in the family before and after the divorce.

Experts agree that divorce may be less traumatic when the child is under 15 months or over 15 years old. In their research on 131 children from 2½ years old to adolescence in divorcing families, Judith Wallerstein and her co-workers concluded that "approximately 15 to 20% of all children whose parents divorce have at least moderate difficulties." Here is what they found in different age groups:

- *Preschoolers*: Toddlers may regress in toilet training or may become more aggressive, irritable, and dependent. Preschool or young school-age children are particularly vulnerable because they may blame themselves, feeling that "Daddy left because I was bad." Yet most return within a year to their previous developmental pace.
- *Early elementary*: These children do not blame themselves or feel guilty. Their primary response is pervasive sadness. First and second graders worry about the divorce's impact on their future and about antagonizing their mothers. About half suffer some decline in school performance; a fourth are worse off psychologically a year after the divorce.
- *Later elementary*: The reactions of school-age children are more complex. Initially they seem to fare better than their younger siblings, but they often feel intense anger. Some become lonely, helpless, and depressed; they may develop psychosomatic illnesses (those caused by mental or emotional distress), or have problems in their friendships. At least half show signs of emotional disturbance a year after the divorce.
- *Adolescents*: Teenagers may try to disguise their shame, to suppress anxiety and depression in several ways. They may experiment with alcohol, drugs, and sex or they

THE FAMILY

may test the limits of parental authority in ways they would not otherwise try. By separating an adolescent from the family as she or he is establishing an adult identity, divorce can disrupt the basic developmental process of that age bracket. However, those teens who had been reasonably stable before the divorce usually bounce back within a year.

These are the opinions of just one team of researchers. Others who work in the field of social welfare think that divorce does the most harm to a child of age 6 or 8 who is just beginning to recognize social structures and must always live with her or his parents' breakup; still others say that a child's age has less to do with the impact of a divorce than does her or his psychological makeup and feelings about each parent.

Single-Parent Families The great majority (89%) of children in single-parent homes live with their mothers. Although the number of families headed by single fathers tripled from 1970 to 1982 to a total of 600,000, that number is still less than 2% of all families with children under 18. More than half of all black children live with a single parent (usually with the mother), as against only 20% of white children.

Most "single parents" have been separated or divorced. However, women who have never married account for the most rapid increase among single-parent families headed by the mother. The median age of single mothers is lower than in the past—34.6 years—largely because of an increase in young, never-married mothers and a higher divorce rate among women who marry at a very young age.

Some single parents suffer that fate as a result of the death of the spouse. As men have a higher rate of early death than women, and because such deaths (from accidents and heart disease, for instance) may come about suddenly, the mother is often left unprepared; the children, too, can feel the shock in forms that may require the help of a family therapist to mend. Insurance compensation and other benefits from good financial planning help the family through their troubled period. And an unexpected death can pull several generations of a family more closely together, as all members try to ease one another through the time of sadness.

More than half of families headed by single mothers have yearly incomes of less than $10,000, which is about half the income of male-headed families. In 1984, 88% of single fathers were em-

THE FAMILY IN TRANSITION

Nuclear Family versus Single-Parent Family

☐ Two-parent family (all races)
▨ Single-parent family (all races)

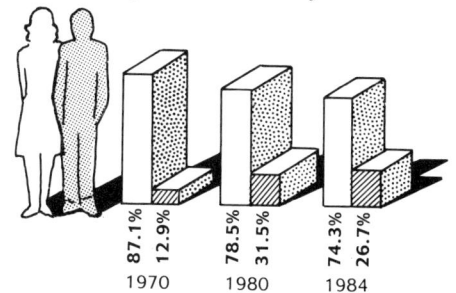

	1970	1980	1984
Two-parent	87.1%	78.5%	74.3%
Single-parent	12.9%	31.5%	26.7%

Female Head of Family
Single-parent family maintained by mother

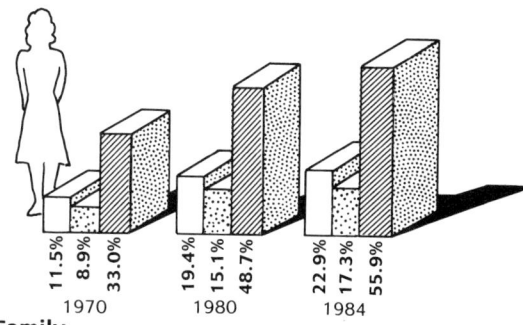

☐ All races
▨ White
▨ Black

	1970	1980	1984
All races	11.5%	19.4%	22.9%
White	8.9%	15.1%	17.3%
Black	33.0%	48.7%	55.9%

Male Head of Family
Single-parent family maintained by father

☐ All races
▨ Black
▨ White

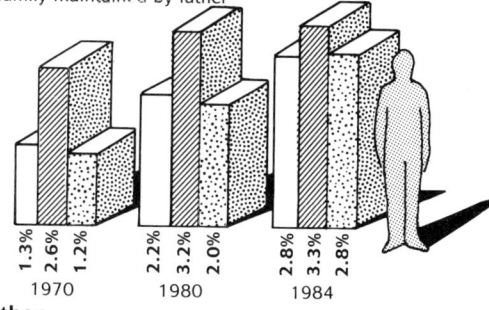

	1970	1980	1984
All races	1.3%	2.2%	2.8%
Black	2.6%	3.2%	3.3%
White	1.2%	2.0%	2.8%

Unmarried Mother
Single-parent maintained by unmarried mother

☐ All races
▨ White
▨ Black

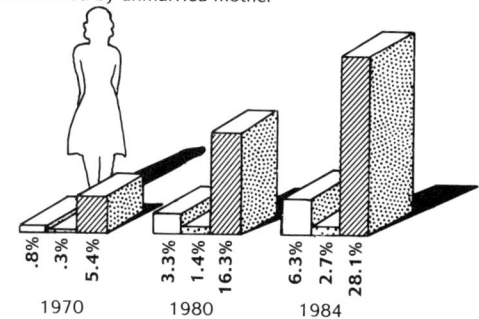

	1970	1980	1984
All races	.8%	3.3%	6.3%
White	.3%	1.4%	2.7%
Black	5.4%	16.3%	28.1%

Source: U.S. Bureau of the Census

THE FAMILY

ployed compared to 69% of single mothers, perhaps in part because single mothers are less likely to have finished high school than are single fathers. Divorced women, and mothers with older children, have higher employment rates than mothers who never married.

Every single-parent family is different from the next, just like other families. An educated divorced woman in her thirties with one school-age child has very different options from a young, unskilled, never-married woman with three preschoolers.

Interestingly, the status of being a single parent does not seem to change some things. At every economic level, the amount of time a single parent spends with his or her children is about the same as the time given to children in a two-parent family. And psychologists have found no negative impact on the intellectual or academic achievement of children from one-parent homes.

Joint Custody

Thirty-three states now have joint custody laws that give children "meaningful and frequent" access to both parents. The positive side of a joint-custody arrangement is that it places the interests of the child before the problems of the parents. The negative side is that having to "share" the kids may bring as much conflict upon the parents as the marriage that preceded it, with the child again caught in the middle.

Psychotherapists are still debating the psychological advantages and disadvantages of joint custody. In one study of 25 joint custody families, psychologist Judith Wallerstein concluded that "there is scant evidence to suggest that joint custody protects the young child against the stress of divorce."

Yet for parents who genuinely want "to divorce their spouses, not their children," joint custody may offer an appealing alternative. And in yet another way, it is changing our definition of the traditional nuclear family.

TEENAGE PREGNANCY: CHILDREN HAVING CHILDREN

Pregnancy and birth rates among teenagers began to decline in the 1980s, but the United States still has the highest rates of adolescent pregnancy and abortion of any developed country.

What Do Families Do Together?

A young family celebrates Halloween together. Family health and intimacy are based on such shared moments, rewarding to both parents and child.

In 1975 and 1981, the Institute for Social Research at the University of Michigan surveyed families (1,500 in 1975, 922 of the same households in 1981) about how they spent their time together. The number-one major recreational pursuit shared by parents and children is watching television.

Television viewing took up about one-fourth of the time parents and children spent together each week. Nonworking mothers spent even more time watching TV with their kids than working mothers: an average of 8 hours per week, versus 6 hours and 40 minutes.

Working mothers spent an average of 11 minutes per weekday and 30 minutes per weekend day on "quality time" activities, such as reading, talking, or playing with children. At-home mothers gave 30 minutes of each weekday and 36 minutes each weekend day to such activities. Fathers spent far less time with their children—an average of 8 minutes per weekday and 14 minutes on weekends.

Parents reading to their children may be the most serious casualty of the television age. Studies have consistently shown that in families in which a regular reading hour is part of the day's activities, the family's bonds are closer and the children perform better in school.

THE FAMILY

Every year approximately 1.1 million teenage girls become pregnant; of these, 45% undergo abortions. Of those who carry to term, 90% keep their babies. Until 30 or 40 years ago, most teenage mothers were married. Today most are not.

Nearly half of the black women in the United States become pregnant by age 20, and the teenage-pregnancy rate among blacks is almost twice what it is among whites. But, while the birthrate among minority teenagers is dropping, the birthrate among white teenagers is rising.

Researchers have linked teenage pregnancy with earlier menarche (onset of menstruation) and increased sexual activity. In a Johns Hopkins University survey of urban adolescents, the average age for first intercourse was 16.2 years for girls and 15.7 for boys. Many adolescents neither know about nor use birth control. In one survey of sexually active girls between ages 15 and 19, only 34% always used birth control; 39% used it occasionally; 27% never used it.

Pregnancy poses health risks for the teenager and her child. She is more likely than an adult to develop complications in pregnancy, and her child is more likely to have a low birth weight and to die in its first year of life. However, some risks can be overcome. According to a study by the National Institute of Child Health and Development, pregnant teenagers who receive adequate prenatal care gain more weight during pregnancy and deliver fewer premature or low-birthweight babies. Yet nearly 1 in 10 adolescents does not start prenatal care until the third trimester or receives none at all.

Pregnancy has other effects on a teenager's life. Adolescents who give birth before completing high school are less likely to finish a degree and more likely to get pregnant again than are teens who do not have children. Without education, they can become trapped in poverty.

Women who were teenage mothers are more likely to be unemployed or to have lower-paying jobs. They also have higher rates of marital separation, divorce, and remarriage. And their children are more likely to become pregnant as teenagers. According to one study, 82% of girls who give birth at age 15 or younger are daughters of teenage mothers.

•   •   •   •

CHAPTER 8

FAMILIES OF THE HEART

Woman with adopted granddaughter

Families can be made as well as born. Children who enter a home through adoption or by a parent's remarriage can forge bonds as strong as those of blood ties. As researchers at the Princeton Center for Infancy note, "It is the caring, not the bearing, that counts."

A family of the heart, in its most general sense, is any home in which people not related by blood live together. The usual forms the setup takes are foster homes and stepfamilies. There is also the "substitute" family, such as a group of adult roommates (usually in their 20s or 30s) who by virtue of strong emotional ties and common interests live together in what they consider a family setting. Whatever the motive, the creation of a family takes

THE FAMILY

time—time to build trust, time to accept differences, time to let love grow.

For years, adoption has been a happy solution for couples who want children and for youngsters who need homes. But while the demand for children has grown, the supply has fallen. The reasons: more effective contraception, legalized abortion, and greater acceptance of unwed motherhood.

FINDING A CHILD

According to the National Committee for Adoption, a nonprofit group, 142,000 to 160,000 adoptions occur in the United States every year. Three-fifths involve stepparents and other relatives who are taking legal responsibility for a child already in the family. That leaves only 50,000 youngsters available for the more than 2,000,000 couples who want to adopt. Some agencies have five- to seven-year waiting lists for would-be parents.

Couples who want to adopt have several options. They can work with public adoption agencies chartered by state governments and supported by tax dollars or with private agencies licensed by the state but not government funded. Concerned groups of parents and religious organizations provide independent adoption services. Private lawyers put infertile couples in touch with unwed pregnant teenagers and arrange independent adoptions. There are also international adoption agencies that specialize in placing infants from South America or Asia in American homes.

In 1985, approximately 25,000 healthy newborns were adopted in the United States, most through independent placements at an average cost of $12,500. With as many as 100 couples vying for each available healthy white infant, more families have looked abroad for children. By 1986, when 6,188 children came from Korea and 2,060 from Latin America, foreign placements were nearly double what they had been in 1981. More than 60% of these babies were less than a year old.

Other New Trends Couples are also adopting more hard-to-place children, including older youngsters and the physically and mentally handicapped. In 1985, more than 14,000 children with special needs were adopted. Transracial adoption (adopting American children of another race) accounts for less than one percent of all adoptions.

Families of the Heart

Traditionally, adoption has represented a break with the genetic past. Records identifying the "birth mother" were sealed. The child might know he or she was adopted but not who the birth parents were. Mothers who put their babies up for adoption were promised that their children would have no way of learning the identity of their natural parents.

In recent years, this tradition has changed. More adopted children have begun looking for their parents and, sometimes, for the brothers and sisters they never knew. Some birth parents also want to find their children, if only to explain why they gave them up. One sociologist explains this almost-desperate need to get in touch with blood relatives as an "effort to overcome a sense of dislocation in a world whose future seems extremely uncertain."

Arguing that it is a human right, if not a constitutional one, to know the identity of one's biological parents, national organizations have lobbied for the release of once-secret records to adoptees. Adopted children may also need to have certain medical information about their natural parents, such as whether they had diabetes. One result has been the development of "open" adoptions, in which records are available to all concerned: the birth mother, the adopting parents, and the child. Some birth mothers in open adoptions arrange for legal, limited contact throughout the child's life.

More and more couples want to adopt a child, but the restrictions are tight and there is a shortage of available children. This woman's three-year wait before getting her Korean son is not an uncommon amount of time.

THE FAMILY

Growing Up Adopted

In the past, parents feared that to tell children they were adopted might be harmful. Today, psychotherapists advise parents to tell children at an early age. Most feel that the children should never be able to remember a time when they did not know they were adopted.

At the age when children begin to ask about where they came from, parents can tell the story of how they found them and other details of their adoption as simply and truthfully as possible. Adoption should be presented as a fact of the child's life, as an interesting but not unusual fact.

Foster Homes

Whereas adoption permanently places a child in a family, foster care is temporary. Children enter a foster home because of some problem that prevents them from staying with their own families. In most cases, they expect to return eventually. The federal government estimates that 276,000 children were in foster care as of 1987.

A couple poses with 3 of their 9 foster children and 3 of their 41 grandchildren. A "family of the heart" can provide all the support a child needs.

The "problem" that makes foster care necessary may be a legal snag in arranging an adoption. Foster care provides a place for the child to stay while the red tape is being untangled. If a mother is a drug abuser, a child may stay in a foster home until the mother completes rehabilitation and demonstrates that she can resume responsibility for the child. Other situations have no clear end in sight, such as an abusive father who refuses treatment.

The basic types of foster care are as follows:

- Emergency: A child is placed in a foster home for no more than 30 days because of a crisis such as a parent's serious illness.
- Limited: The arrangement is temporary, but the length of time is uncertain. The child will return to the biological parents when they are ready to resume their responsibilities.
- Preadoptive: The child will be adopted by the foster family as soon as the biological parents' rights are terminated.
- Permanent: Although legal or medical problems prevent adoption, the child will not be able to return to the birth parents' home.
- Specialized: The children in these cases are usually disabled, seriously ill, part of a family group, or unmarried teenagers with babies.

Foster care is subject to federal, state, and local laws. Families must undergo a study to determine if they are capable of providing foster care. If an agency determines a family is suitable (taking into consideration the family's income, attitudes, stability, and other information), it automatically issues a license. Once a child is placed in a home, a family will have to see the agency caseworkers and will receive payments for the child's support.

STEPFAMILIES

Stepfamilies, sometimes called "blended" families, are those in which at least one spouse was previously married and has children. Divorce sets the stage for the creation of most of today's stepfamilies. Others form after one parent dies and the other remarries.

Though previously frowned upon, this kind of household is now part of mainstream life in the United States. About 1 in every 10 children lives with a stepparent, and the estimate is that 1 in 4 will live in a stepfamily before turning 18.

Stepfamilies are usually neither as ideal as television's ever-perky "Brady Bunch" nor as cruel as the evil stepparents in fairy tales. In fact, growing research suggests that stepfamilies on the whole are no worse and no better than conventional nuclear families.

Yet they are different. As Vance Packard observes in *Our Endangered Children*, "Stepfamilies simply cannot operate like traditional families—at least not for quite a while. It takes more ingenuity, flexibility, and dedication to make a second marriage work."

In a traditional family, the couple comes together to have a child, and the child is part of both of them, pulling them closer. Those forces work against stepfamilies, as the old blood ties may pull the family in opposite directions. In the beginning, a stepfamily may actually function like two single-parent families, with the children clustering around their "real" parent.

Having to deal with living former spouses can add to the tensions between a new couple, but the issues stepfamilies must deal with are essentially the same, regardless of why a previous marriage ended. After either divorce or death, children mourn for the family they lost and resist making the commitment to stepparents who threaten to replace the parents they knew and loved.

Usually the first year is the hardest. Virtual strangers are expected to live together like a family before they feel like a family. Each family member may have different problems adjusting. The spouses may long for some "couple" time just for themselves or argue over the rules of each other's "ex." The children may resent their new parent, dislike their new siblings, or miss their old family, house, friends, and neighborhood. Every aspect of family life—discipline, chores, finances, traditions, mealtimes, vacations—may have to be negotiated.

A stepfamily's success in finding compromises and solving problems depends on several factors: the commitment of the couple, the ages and sexes of the children, the relationships with former spouses, and whether the couple decides to have children of their own.

Growing Up a Stepchild Some experts feel that young children (under three) and older teenagers find it easiest to join a new family. The most difficult ages seem to be between 9 and 15, when children are approaching or going through puberty and making moves toward independence.

Almost all stepchildren feel torn between their biological parents and their stepparents. Often they worry that loving a stepparent is a betrayal of the biological parent. Only with time can they make room in their hearts to love both.

The Stepfamily Foundation of America offers this advice, called "Steps for Steps," to help blended families make it through the difficult first months:

- Recognize that a stepfamily will not and cannot function as a natural family. It has its own special set of dynamics and behaviors.
- Do not try to be a "super stepparent"—it does not work. The advice to stepparents: Go slow.

The children of divorced families may be torn between loyalty to a natural parent and to the stepparent. The conflict can take years to resolve.

- Recognize that a stepfamily will not and cannot function as a natural family. It has its own special set of dynamics and behaviors.
- Do not try to be a "super stepparent"—it does not work. The advice to stepparents: Go slow.
- Establish clear job descriptions among parent, stepparent, and children.
- Talk through each member's expectations on subjects such as money, discipline, the prior spouse, emotional support, etc.
- Remember there are no ex-parents, just ex-spouses. Although it may be difficult, maintaining civility between the old and new families is worth the effort.
- Recognize that a conflict of loyalties is normal for children torn between people they love.

Just as most children usually come to accept and love their stepparents, most stepparents learn their share of lessons. As the writer John Leonard put it, "Having become a stepfather, I think I am a better father to my own children than I was when, as an amateur, I didn't have time to listen to them and I thought they owed me something. We owe them something: their dignity. Then maybe they will love us."

• • • •

CHAPTER 9

CHALLENGES FOR TODAY'S FAMILIES

Parenthood demands the best in two people. Inevitably, it sometimes brings out the worst. Perhaps the most any parent can do is let common sense be the guide. That, plus love for each other and for the children within their family, is the timeless basis for parenting in any age or circumstance.

Two-career couples now head 2 out of 3 families with children under 18. More than 60% of women with children under age 18 work—a dramatic increase from the 1960s, when only 30% of mothers worked outside the home. The days of a mother who stays at home are not over, nor are the days when all fathers

THE FAMILY

went to work. Though house husbands number only in the thousands, they are among a growing number of men who have decided that their principal satisfaction in life can be raising the kids. Balancing jobs and childrearing is a task all families have had to learn how to perform, and today the options are more numerous.

Women and Work

Most wives work to help make financial ends meet, but their jobs may have other benefits for them. Work can bring them new challenges and satisfactions. In extensive studies on health and social roles, Dr. Lois Verbrugge at the University of Michigan has found that working wives and mothers are healthier and happier—though often more hassled—than women who do not work outside their homes. Yet many working mothers feel anxious, even guilty about their careers.

"These days you're damned if you work and damned if you don't," says Sandra Scarr, a mother of four, chairperson of the psychology department at the University of Virginia and author of Mother Care/Other Care. "Scratch the surface of a working mother, and she's worried about doing the best thing for her children. Scratch the surface of a nonworking mother, and she's worried about the world passing her by."

More dual-career couples are starting their families later in life. This gives both partners a chance to establish themselves professionally before they take on the responsibilities of raising a child.

A day-care center in Chicago tends to the children of teenage mothers who want to continue their education. Facilities such as this one enable women to enter the job market and lead independent lives.

The Impact on Children Do the children of working mothers suffer? That question has sparked intense debate. Jay Belsky, a professor of human development at Pennsylvania State University, set off a firestorm of controversy by reporting in 1986 that infants less than a year old who receive more than 20 hours of nonmaternal care a week are more likely to have insecure relationships with their parents. Studies have shown that such "insecure" children later develop behavior problems, such as aggressiveness.

Other researchers have disputed Belsky's findings about early day-care. And almost all, including Belsky, agree that after the first year there are no significant differences between children cared for at home or elsewhere.

For older children, a working mother may be even more of a plus. A nationwide study by Ohio psychologists of the impact of maternal employment found that school-age children with working mothers not only survive but thrive, outperforming classmates with at-home mothers academically, behaviorally, and socially. Among the key findings in the myth-shattering investigation are as follows.

School-age children with working mothers have higher IQs, get better grades, and earn higher ratings from their teachers than those with nonworking mothers. They also develop better communication skills and score higher on tests of self-reliance.

Children whose mothers have part-time jobs (or work fewer than 40 hours a week), though, seem to have the best of both worlds. These children score higher than their peers whose mothers work full-time and higher than children whose mothers did not work. It is not part-time work alone that accounts for this benefit to the children—many social and economic factors come into play to explain it.

Nonetheless, at all income levels, the children of working mothers showed clear advantages. The higher the family income and the mother's occupational status, the more the children benefitted.

When parents were divorced, the children whose mothers worked got better grades, showed more originality and involvement in classroom activities, and had more hobbies and interests than students with nonworking single mothers.

Homosexuality

Homosexuality is no longer defined as a mental illness, but it remains a difficult issue for families to confront. No one knows how many parents and spouses are bisexual (sexual proclivity toward both women and men). Because society has become more accepting of homosexuality over the last 20 years, homosexuals and bisexuals may feel less pressure to hide their sexual preference. If a bisexual or homosexual parent decides to "come out" by announcing his or her sexual preference, the parent and his or her children have to come to terms with the impact sexual preference may have on the family. Lesbianism and bisexuality in women are thought to occur less often, though fewer studies have been conducted on these topics.

Some bisexuals and homosexuals remain married and involved in family life; others leave their families to live with their homosexual partners. Gay couples have been granted custody of one partner's children by a previous marriage. In these cases, the judge will usually weigh not a person's sexual preference but his or her ability to provide a loving, stable home for the youngster.

By some estimates, nearly one of every three men has a homosexual encounter during the late teen years. Male homosexuals

Challenges for Today's Families

recall becoming aware of their attraction to other men at about age 13, but most did not think of themselves as gay until at least age 19.

Some homosexual boys and girls, in part because of society's homophobia, are under enormous pressure from themselves and from society to be "just like everyone else"—not necessarily heterosexual, but at least accepted. One study, reported in the July 10, 1987, issue of the *Journal of the American Medical Association*, found that 40% of gay young men had consulted psychiatrists, and that 31% had attempted suicide.

Today, young homosexual men face another dilemma: the risk of AIDS (acquired immune deficiency syndrome), which can be spread between men through homosexual contact. AIDS is also a risk to any man or woman who has sexual intercourse with a partner who has practiced unsafe sex or has shared needles with intravenous-drug users.

Domestic Violence in the United States

The Federal Bureau of Investigation considers domestic violence the most common and least-reported crime in the United States. One-third of all murders in the United States occur within the family.

Spouse Abuse Battered wives outnumber battered husbands by a ratio of 10 to 1. According to FBI estimates, a woman is physically abused every 18 seconds; women have a 50% chance of being hit at least once by their husbands or lovers. The primary factors contributing to spouse abuse are frustration and stress, alcohol (involved in up to 60% of batterings), and whether the spouse himself or herself was raised in a home in which abuse occurred.

Only 1 in 20 men who beat their wives is violent outside the home; 9 in 10 refuse to admit they have a problem. The National Council on Child Abuse and Neglect estimates that in homes where the wife is beaten, 30 to 70% of the children are also abused.

Child Abuse Severe child abuse occurs an estimated 1,700,000 times a year, leading to the deaths of as many as 2,000 children. Child abuse occurs in every economic, social, educational, religious, and racial group, and it takes many forms: physical abuse, physical neglect, emotional abuse, emotional neglect, verbal abuse, and sexual abuse.

Joel Steinberg (left) and Hedda Nussbaum (right) were arrested in 1987 for the murder of their adopted daughter. Child abuse is a widening national concern.

According to one clinical study, only 10% of abusive parents have psychiatric disorders. But as children, most felt misunderstood, unrewarded, criticized. In many ways, they were denied the right to behave like children. Sometimes they were abused themselves; even if they were not physically harmed, they grew up feeling so worthless and unlovable that they continue to search for mothering and love.

Such individuals often marry someone with problems similar to their own. When the new relationship cannot meet their psychological needs, they feel rejected. To them, children may seem the last resort for giving them the love they crave. When they do not live up to these expectations, children become victims of abuse.

Approximately 70 to 75% of abusive families can be helped with appropriate treatment. Usually that involves counseling the entire family. Within the family structure, abusive parents must learn to view their children realistically and to cope in positive rather than negative ways.

Challenges for Today's Families

Incest

Incest means sexual relations between individuals too closely related to contract a legal marriage. Taboos against incest may or may not extend to aunts, uncles, and cousins.

In one national study, 15% of the respondents reported some sexual contact with relatives; 7% reported intercourse with relatives. The most common form of incest is between teenage brothers and sisters and cannot be considered in the same criminal category as child molestation or rape.

Unfortunately, when incest occurs between a father or another adult male relative and a young child, the child may find it impossible to convince the other parent of the truth. Parents often cannot handle the emotional trauma of finding out that some adult they love—brother, husband, son, grandfather—would "do that." The child, then, is not only sexually abused but rejected by those he or she turns to for protection.

Children of Alcoholics

Alcoholism and drug use shatters families, and often the children suffer the most, physically and psychologically.

There are 28 million children of alcoholics; about 7 million are under 18. Sons of alcoholics are four times more likely to become alcoholics than are other male children. Daughters of alcoholic mothers are three times more likely to become alcoholics than other daughters.

Drinking contributes to 38% of cases of child abuse. Alcoholism is involved, directly or indirectly, in 40% of the problems brought to family courts. Alcoholics' children also are more prone to learning disorders, anorexia nervosa (willful starvation and a mania about thinness), frantic overachievement, and suicide.

Children of alcoholics are often forced to adopt certain roles:

- The "lost child" or adjuster who does whatever the parent wants without thinking.
- The "family hero" who takes over many household tasks.
- The "peacemaker" who worries constantly about the family's pain.
- The "scapegoat" who shows anger by causing trouble at home or in school.
- The "mascot" who defuses tension by clowning.

THE FAMILY

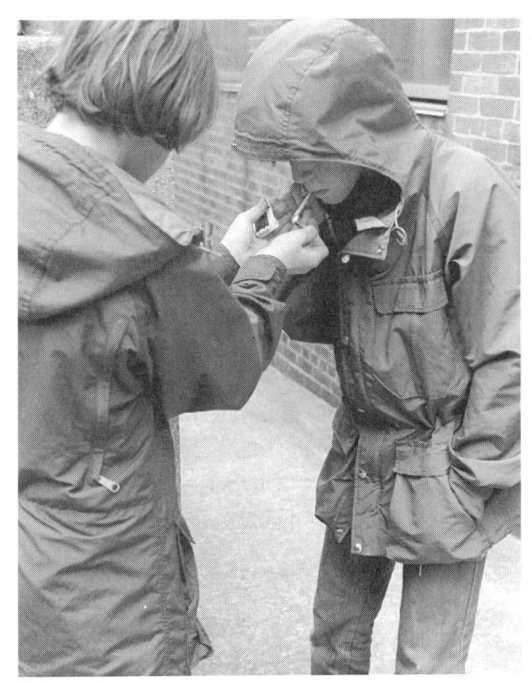

Adolescents sometimes use drugs to defy their parents or to cope with domestic tension. When any member of a family has a drug or alcohol problem, the chances escalate that violence and discord will occur.

Illness

The way families respond to illness are strikingly similar. "The psychological issues are the same, whether the problem is back injury, diabetes, or depression," says psychologist JoAnne LeMaistre, author of *Beyond Rage*. Typically, families make the same mistake: Trying to do everything they can for a sick parent or child, they end up doing too little for each other and themselves.

In her studies of helpful and unhelpful support, social psychologist Camille Wortman of the University of Michigan found that "excessive involvement and attempting to do too much are more common sources of difficulty than insufficient involvement and inattention." In other words, the relative who tries to play doctor or psychologist can do more harm than the relative who seems not to care.

A child's illness or disability places enormous strain on a family. Mothers of children with severe physical or mental handicaps consistently show greater stress than those with normal, healthy children. Increasingly, health professionals are providing support groups for families of the disabled and recommending psycho-

Challenges for Today's Families

logical counseling for the entire family as well as medical treatment for the young patient with a chronic medical problem, such as diabetes, asthma, or anorexia nervosa.

Teenage Drinking and Drug Abuse

Alcoholism and drug abuse are problems not only for adults. About 30% of teenagers experience negative consequences from drinking, including alcohol-related accidents, arrests, or impaired health or school performance.

By the time they reach their twenties, 80% of young adults have tried an illegal drug. Young people between the ages of 14 and 24 are the most likely to experiment with drugs. Some are lucky enough to satisfy their curiosity without getting hurt or caught. Others pay a terrible price. They lose their self-esteem, their health, their friends, and sometimes even their families. And those who share needles for using intravenous drugs run a high risk of exposing themselves to the AIDS virus, thereby trading in their lives.

Teenagers may turn to drugs to defy their parents or escape from other problems at home. If drugs become the focus of their

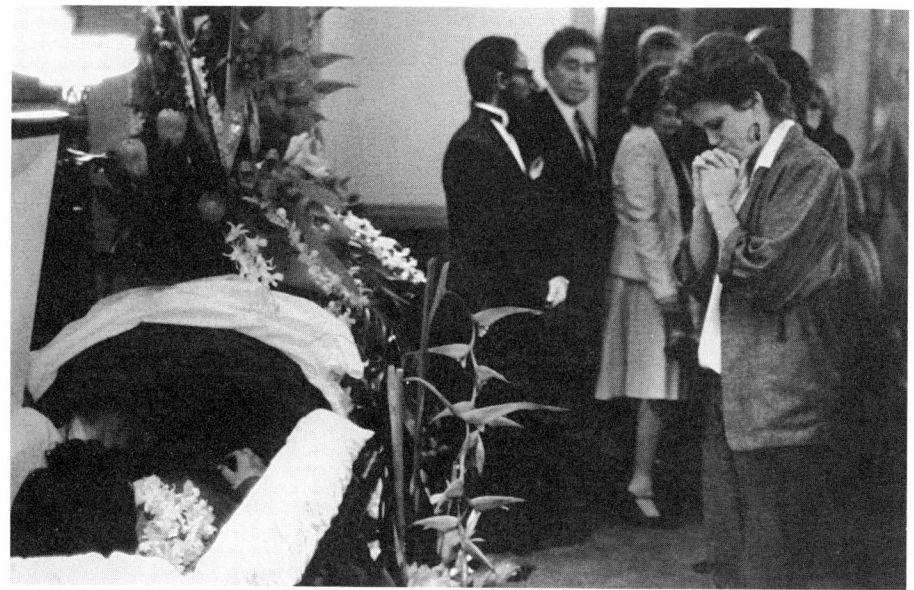

A teenager prays beside the open casket of a schoolmate killed in a drunk-driving car accident. Traffic accidents are responsible for 45% of all teenage deaths each year; at least 60% of these victims are under the influence of alcohol.

THE FAMILY

lives, their families pay a price. One parent may feel guilty for not providing enough love and understanding. The other is angry and wants to enforce more discipline.

By the time a drug user reaches the point of requiring treatment to get off drugs or stop drinking, family therapy is crucial. Everyone in the home must learn new ways of relating to each other and rebuilding trust.

The challenges to the family are enormous, yet it is enormous love and bonding that bring them together in the first place. Whether by working mothers, working fathers, violence, illness, drug abuse, or just the interference of the outside world, the family's resilience is tested each day. What are the family's prospects for the near future?

• • • •

CHAPTER 10

FAMILIES OF THE FUTURE

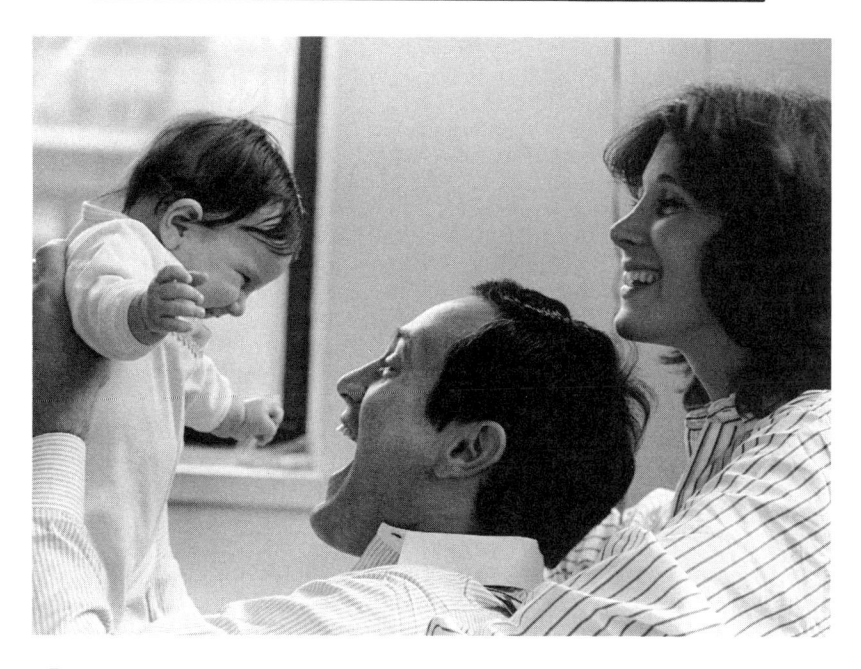

Some sociologists, anthropologists, and psychologists see today's family as a battered institution. They view it as overburdened, undernourished, bloodied by past battles, unprepared for future skirmishes. Others hold just the opposite view: They contend that families are not dying but rather being reborn in new forms and styles.

As one researcher put it, "The family has met fire, flood, famine, earthquake, war, economic and political collapses over the centuries by changing its form, its size, its behavior, its location, its environment, its reality. It is the most resilient social form available to humans."

THE FAMILY

Avid young readers at work in their school library. Educators stress that children from homes where reading is an integral part of daily life have a good head start in their early classroom education.

What will happen to this ever-evolving social institution in the future? We cannot predict the exact shape of anything so central to our culture, but we can extrapolate some current trends. Here is what some experts say we might expect.

Better Marriages, Fewer Kids?

Over the last few centuries, families in Western culture have been getting smaller. In Europe and North America in the mid-1600s, households averaged seven or eight members. Today in America the average number is 2.69, and the government predicts that by 1995 the average household will include just 2.3 persons.

There is no reason to think smaller families will be any less happy. In fact, the children may have an advantage: Educators report that children in small families score higher on IQ and other standardized achievement tests, complete more years of education, and end up with higher-paying jobs than those from large families.

Families of the Future

Young men and women are waiting longer to marry. The average age for first-time spouses was 23.3 years in 1985, compared to 21.1 in 1975. Older first-time brides and grooms tend to have longer-lasting unions. The most likely candidates for divorce are women who marry in their teens or give birth within seven months of their wedding.

The rate of cohabitating couples (those who live together unmarried) nearly quadrupled during the 1970s, but the increase slowed sharply after 1980, and the rate leveled off between 1982 and 1983. The popularity of this kind of living arrangement sparked the invention of many amusing terms trying to describe just what mold these people fit: there are POSSLQ's (Persons of the Opposite Sex Sharing Living Quarters) and unmarried DINK's (Double Income, No Kids), the Sin-in-Law, and the Live-in Lover. Some sociologists predict that this life-style has peaked and will either stay at the present level or decline.

Even with fewer divorces and remarriages, the number of stepfamilies is sure to grow, too. Estimates range from 25% to almost 35% for the number of children who may live with a stepparent before they reach age 18.

Couples with two incomes and no children will flourish in the coming decade. Their biggest single distinction is that they can spend a much greater percentage of their income as they please—be it on travel, cars, a house, clothing, or charity.

Those men and women born between 1965 and 1980, when the birthrate plummeted after the baby boom of 1946–64, will face very different social and economic realities from the baby boomers who preceded them. Because of greater economic and professional opportunities, they may not face the same competition. Marriage prospects should improve, especially for women. And when the children of that era do marry, they may have longer-lasting marriages than their parents because they will marry at a later age and because of their firsthand experience as children or friends of children from broken homes.

Husbands and wives will not necessarily live under the same roof in the future. More couples, particularly those in the middle and upper income brackets, will work in different cities and commute to see each other on weekends. The financial and emotional costs of such arrangements are high, but a University of Maryland psychologist who studied 50 commuting couples found that their divorce rate was only 10%, far below the rate for partners who live together. Though these people will always be a very small part of the U.S. citizenry, they indicate the strength and elasticity of the family as an institution, one that expands to fill all kinds of individual needs.

Or No Marriage, Too Many Kids?

The increase in never-married women, particularly teenagers, who have children, and in divorced women who do not remarry means that more children will grow up in homes with only one parent. Particularly for unwed teenage mothers, the result could be lifelong poverty.

In general, it looks as though there will be a greater gap between the well-off and the needy. There are several economic and political reasons for this polarization, but one of the clearest gaps exists between wed mothers and unwed mothers. Despite the increased opportunities in recent years for women to hold well-paying jobs, that improvement does not make up for the expense of having children—assuming the woman has time to hold a job. For all too many unwed mothers, skimpy welfare checks or living with their parents will be the rule.

Worldwide Trends

Developed nations, which accounted for 22% of the world's population in 1950, now account for 15%. By the year 2030, only 9% of the people in the world will live in developed countries.

Some political experts are warning that a "birth dearth" in developed nations may jeopardize world balance in the next century. The Soviet Union, for one, is very worried that a declining birthrate in its industrialized regions will leave too few people to work its factories, farms, offices, and army by the 1990s. A more international perspective of the same problem would suggest that as the Soviet Union, Canada, United States, Western Europe, Australia, and Japan account for an ever-shrinking proportion of the world's population, those nations' political, military, and cultural influence may fade.

Population growth in Third World countries continues apace. In the 1970s, many countries in Africa, Asia, and South America found that their population growth was outpacing their economic development, and in some cases this is still true. Kenya, if it maintains its population growth rate at 4.1%, the highest in the world, will see its populace double every 20 years. The result is a steady decline in income and living standards, including more widespread poverty and hunger. Government leaders in many underdeveloped nations are considering a one-child-per-family policy, similar to that adopted by China in 1979. There are signs, though, that the population growth rate in some Third World nations is declining to the level of some industrialized nations, around 1 or 2%.

Particularly in developed, industrialized countries, families—and their problems—are becoming increasingly similar. Although the birthrate has dropped in Europe and the United States, the divorce rate has soared. In the Soviet Union, with its very different form of government yet often-similar social patterns, the birthrate fell by 50% from 1939 to 1979, while the divorce rate has skyrocketed by 200% since 1963. Two-thirds of these divorces are initiated by wives—most of whom work and no longer depend on their husbands for support.

Anthropologist Margaret Mead's research of people from all over the world led her to conclude that it is within the family that the child learns his or her formative and most crucial lessons about the self and the world.

THE FAMILY

Even in Japan, where the traditional patriarchal family endured until World War II, the law now acknowledges the equality of the sexes, allowing wives to divorce their husbands and giving them an equal share of family property. In the last 25 years, the divorce rate has doubled. More than half of Japanese women over age 15 work, and about 57% of working women are married—though it should be noted that women in Japan have virtually no real influence in the business world, despite their presence in the workplace.

Yet the more families change, the more they fundamentally remain the same. As the anthropologist Margaret Mead wrote in *Family*, it is within the family—now and in the future—that a child "learns what it means to be a boy or a girl, another person like or different from himself, what it means to be young and weak, growing and maturing, obedient and rebellious, possessive and generous, responsible and careless . . . it is the family within which the child learns about his own and the world's potentialities."

The family is—and will always be—our link to the past, the key to our survival in the present, and our legacy to the future.

•   •   •   •

APPENDIX: FOR MORE INFORMATION

ADOPTION

Committee for Single Adoptive Parents
P.O. Box 15084
Chevy Chase, MD 20815

North American Council on Adoptable Children
P.O. Box 14808
Minneapolis, MN 55414

For information on adopting children from either domestic or foreign countries or counseling referrals for prospective adoptive parents, contact:

International Concerns Committee for Children
AnnaMarie Merrill
911 Cypress Drive
Boulder, CO 80303

ALCOHOLISM

Check your telephone book for the local chapter of Alcoholics Anonymous, Al-Anon, or Alateen, or contact:

Al-Anon Family Group Headquarters
200 Park Avenue South
New York, NY 10010
(212) 254-7230

Alcohol/Drug Abuse Referral hotline (800) ALC-OHOL, 24 hours a day

Alcoholics Anonymous
468 Park Avenue South
New York, NY 10016
(212) 686-1100

Children of Alcoholics Foundation
200 Park Avenue, 31st Floor
New York, NY 10166
(212) 351-2680

National Clearing House for Alcohol Information
Box 2345
Rockville, MD 20852

National Council on Alcoholism, Inc.
12 West 21st Street, 7th Floor
New York, NY 10010
(212) 206-6770

THE FAMILY

BIRTH CONTROL

Planned Parenthood Federation of America, Inc.
810 Seventh Avenue
New York, NY 10019
(212) 541-7800

(Planned Parenthood can also provide information about sexually transmitted diseases, pregnancy, and basic gynecological care.) Consult your telephone directory for a local chapter.

BIRTH DEFECTS

The National Foundation—March of Dimes
1275 Mamaroneck Avenue
White Plains, NY 10605
(914) 428-7100

CHILD/SEXUAL ABUSE

Child abuse reporting center
(800) 342-3720

Childhelp
P.O. Box 630
Hollywood, CA 90028

Family violence/child abuse hotline
(800) 422-4453, 24 hours a day

Parents Anonymous
2810 Artesia Boulevard
Redondo Beach, CA 90278
(Referrals to local groups available from above address.)

Rape hotline (202) 333-RAPE, 24 hours a day (check your telephone directory—usually the first page—for a local rape hotline)

DISEASE INFORMATION

National Health Information Clearinghouse (800) 336-4797 (referrals to sources of information on specific topics)

National Self-help Clearing House
33 West 42nd Street
New York, NY 10036

DRUG ABUSE

Addicts Anonymous
P.O. Box 200
Lexington, KY 40507

Drug abuse hotline (800) 548-3008, 24 hours a day

National Institute on Drug Abuse hotline (800) 662-HELP

HOMOSEXUALITY

Gay Switchboard hotline (national referrals)—(215) 464-7485

Institute for the Protection of Lesbian and Gay Youth, Inc.
401 West Street
New York, NY 10014
(212) 633-8920

National Federation of Parents and Friends of Gays
8020 Eastern Avenue, N.W.
Washington, DC 20012
(202) 726-3223

PARENTHOOD

American Family Society
Washington, DC 20088
(202) 460-4455

Appendix: For More Information

National Association Concerned
 with School-Age Parents
7315 Wisconsin Avenue
Suite 211-W
Washington, DC 20014

PREGNANCY

Check your phone book under city, county, or state for Department of Health listings for maternal and child health, or maternity services and family planning. These bureaus may be able to provide information on locally available prenatal care, counseling, or childbirth classes.

For information on abortion:

National Abortion Federation
900 Pennsylvania Avenue, S.E.
Washington, DC 20003
(202) 546-9060
hotline (800) 772-9100

For information on pregnancy and genetic counseling, contact:

National Maternal and Child Health
 Clearinghouse
3520 Prospect Street, N.W.
Washington, DC 20057
(202) 625-8410

SEXUALLY TRANSMITTED DISEASES

AIDS hotline (800) 342-AIDS—
 recorded general information
 (800) 447-AIDS—U.S. Public
 Health Service

National Sexually Transmitted
 Diseases hotline (800) 227-8922

For free booklets on AIDS, chlamydia, herpes, genital warts, and the transmission of disease during pregnancy, contact:

American Social Health Association
260 Sheridan Avenue
Palo Alto, CA 94306

FURTHER READING

Ariès, Philippe. *Centuries of Childhood: A Social History of Family Life.* New York: Random House, 1965.

Bank, Stephen P., and Michael D. Kahn. *The Sibling Bond.* New York: Basic Books, 1982.

Barker, Philip. *Basic Family Therapy.* 2nd ed. New York: Oxford University Press, 1984.

Bell, Ruth. *Changing Bodies, Changing Lives.* New York: Random House, 1980.

Bolles, Edmund Blair. *The Penguin Adoption Handbook.* New York: Penguin Books, 1984.

Brubaker, Timothy H. *Later Life Families.* Beverly Hills, CA: Sage, 1985.

Cox, Frank D. *Human Intimacy & Marriage, the Family and Its Meanings.* St. Paul: West, 1984.

DuVall, E. M., and Brent Miller, eds. *Marriage and Family Development.* New York: Harper & Row, 1985.

Furstenberg, Frank F., Jr., and Graham B. Spanier. *Recycling the Family.* Beverly Hills, CA: Sage, 1987.

Garver, Kenneth L., and Sandra Marchese. *Genetic Counseling for Clinicians.* Chicago: Year Book Medical Publishers, 1986.

Goldenberg, Irene, and Herbert Goldenberg. *Family Therapy: An Overview.* 2nd ed. Monterey, CA: Brooks/Cole, 1985.

Goldthorpe, J. E. *Family Life in Western Societies.* Cambridge: Cambridge University Press, 1987.

Hansen, James C., ed. *Cultural Perspectives in Family Therapy.* Rockville, MD: Aspen, 1983.

Howard, Jane. *Families.* New York: Simon & Schuster, 1987.

Kelly, Thaddeus E. *Clinical Genetics and Genetic Counseling.* 2nd ed. Chicago: Year Book Medical Publishers, 1986.

Further Reading

Kottak, Conrad Phillip. *Anthropology: The Exploration of Human Diversity.* 3rd ed. New York: Random House, 1982.

Lamb, Michael E. *Nontraditional Families: Parenting and Child Development.* Hillsdale, NJ: Lawrence Erlbaum Associates, 1982.

Leman, Kevin. *The Birth Order Book.* New York: Dell, 1985.

Leslie, Gerald, and Sheila Korman. *The Family in Social Context.* New York: Oxford University Press, 1985.

Levande, Diane et al. *Marriage and the Family.* Boston: Houghton-Mifflin, 1983.

McCoy, Kathy, and Charles Wibbelsman, M.D. *The New Teenage Body Book.* Los Angeles: The Body Press, 1987.

Macklin, Eleanor, and Roger Rubin. *Contemporary Families and Alternative Lifestyles.* Beverly Hills, CA: Sage, 1983.

Mead, Margaret, and Ken Heyman. *Family.* New York: Macmillan, 1965.

Mintz, Steven, and Susan Kellogg. *A Social History of American Family Life.* New York: Free Press, 1987.

National Genetics Foundation. *Clinical Genetics Handbook.* Oradell, NJ: Medical Economics Books, 1987.

Packard, Vance. *Our Endangered Children: Growing Up in a Changing World.* Boston: Little, Brown, 1983.

Segalen, Martine. *Historical Anthropology of the Family.* Cambridge: Cambridge University Press, 1986.

Stinnett, Nick, and John DeFrain. *Secrets of Strong Families.* Boston: Little, Brown, 1985.

Strong, Brian, and Christine DeVault. *The Marriage and Family Experience.* 3rd ed. St. Paul: West, 1986.

GLOSSARY

amniocentesis a test for genetic defects in an unborn child; chromosomes in fetal cells drawn from fluid inside the amnion (one of the membranes surrounding the fetus) are examined for abnormality; cannot be performed until 14 to 16 weeks into a pregnancy

barrier contraceptive a form of birth control such as a diaphragm, cervical cap, or condom that blocks the meeting of egg and sperm by means of a physical barrier

cervical cap a form of contraception consisting of a rubber or plastic cap, which resembles a large thimble and fits snugly around the cervix; it blocks the path of sperm to the uterus

cervix narrow pathway that connects the uterus to the vagina

chlamydia a very common sexually transmitted disease; it can lead to pelvic inflammatory disease, which may cause sterility; treatable with antibiotics

chorionic villi sampling method of testing for genetic defects very early in a pregnancy (8 to 10 weeks); the chromosomes in cells taken from the chorion (one of the membranes surrounding the embryo) are examined for abnormality

chromosomes the rodlike structures found in the nucleus of mammalian cells that contain the genes; each human cell (except gametes) contains 23 pairs of chromosomes

clan a group of kinsmen related in different ways in different societies; in some societies a clan is made up of families that trace descent from a common ancestor; in others, it includes all persons with a common surname tracing descent from a common ancestor

condom a sheath, usually made of latex, that covers the penis during sexual intercourse as protection against pregnancy and/or disease; not 100% effective against either, but very effective when used in conjunction with a spermicide containing at least 5% nonoxynol-9

conception the initiation of pregnancy; occurs when female egg cell is fertilized by male sperm cell

Glossary

contraceptive sponge a form of contraception consisting of a soft, disposable polyurethane sponge, about two inches in diameter, saturated with a spermicide

DES diethylstilbestrol; a synthetic estrogen given to pregnant women to prevent miscarriage; has been shown to increase risk of some cancers in daughters of women who took it; use was stopped in 1972

diaphragm a form of contraception consisting of a bowllike rubber cup with a spring rim, in sizes ranging from two to four inches in diameter; holds spermicide and prevents sperm from passing the cervix

diploid number term for the two sets of 23 chromosomes within most cells (the exception being gametes, which contain only one set of 23)

DNA deoxyribonucleic acid; genetic material, composed of paired nitrogenous bases, that contains the chemical instructions for determining an organism's inherited characteristics

embryo the developing fertilized egg during the first eight weeks after conception

estrogen female sex hormone produced by the ovaries; a common ingredient in oral contraceptives

ethnicity the unique characteristics of a cultural subgroup

extended family a family that includes relatives other than parents and children, such as grandparents or cousins

family a group of people united by marriage, blood, or adoption, constituting a single household, interacting and communicating with each other, and creating and maintaining a common culture

family of orientation the family that one is born into

family of procreation the family that a couple forms by marriage

fetus the developing embryo during the period beginning in the ninth week after conception

gametes egg and sperm cells; contain 23 chromosomes rather than 46

genes complex units of chemical material—contained on the chromosomes in cells—that are responsible for inherited traits such as gender or eye color

haploid number term for each set of 23 chromosomes

hemoglobin the component in red blood cells that attaches to oxygen molecules carrying them through the bloodstream

heterosexual a person whose sexual desire is directed toward members of the opposite sex

THE FAMILY

heterozygous a hybrid gene pair containing two genes that code differently for the same trait

homosexual a person whose sexual desire is directed toward members of the same sex

homozygous a gene pair containing two genes that code identically for the same trait

hormone a substance carried in the bloodstream that regulates many bodily processes, modifying both structure and function

incest sexual relations between close relatives

IUD intrauterine device; a small piece of molded plastic with a string attached that is inserted by a physician into the uterus through the cervix; prevents pregnancy by stopping implantation of a fertilized egg

joint custody an arrangement between divorced spouses in which children have "meaningful and frequent" access to both parents

legitimacy social principle by which children born to a married couple have certain rights (including the rights to inherit their parents' property), and the husband, whether or not he is the biological father, serves as their protector, guardian, and link to society

matriarchal families that vest power and authority in females

matrilineal families that pass on property and family name through the mother

menstruation the monthly discharge of blood and cells from the uterine lining that occurs, between puberty and menopause, in women who are not pregnant

monogamy the practice of having only one mate at a time

nuclear family a family that consists of members of two generations: for example, two parents and a child; a single parent and a child; a couple with several adopted or foster children

open adoptions adoptions in which records are open to all concerned: the birth mother, the adopting parents, and the child

oral contraceptives birth control pills; they usually contain a combination of natural or synthetic female sex hormones that prevent pregnancy by preventing ovulation

ovulation release of an egg cell, or ovum, from the ovaries; the time at which a woman is most likely to become pregnant

patriarchal families that vest power and authority in males

Glossary

patrilineal families that pass on property and family name through the father

PID pelvic inflammatory disease; a potentially fatal infection that can occur in women; scar tissue caused by PID is responsible for sterility in a great number of women

polygamy the practice of having more than one mate at a time

progesterone a female sex hormone; plays an important role in the regulation of the menstrual cycle

progestine a synthetic progesteronelike hormone; a common ingredient in oral contraceptives

rhythm method a form of contraception consisting of abstinence from intercourse during the fertile time of the menstrual cycle, that is, during the days preceding and just following ovulation

sib in ancient Israel, a group of kinsmen related through the husbands and fathers

single-parent family family headed by one parent who has never married or who is alone because of death, divorce, or desertion

spermicides chemical foams, creams, jellies, vaginal suppositories, and gels that kill sperm cells and some organisms that cause sexually transmitted diseases

sterilization surgery that affects a person's reproductive capability; the most common sterilization operation for women involves blocking or tying the fallopian tubes (tubal ligation or occlusion); male sterilization is called vasectomy

syphilis a chronic sexually transmitted disease that, if left untreated, can lead to serious physical problems or even death; it can be treated in its early stages with antibiotics

TSS toxic shock syndrome; a potentially fatal disease that strikes women; it has most often been connected with a specific brand of tampon, which is no longer on the market

uterus pear-shaped organ in a woman; in pregnancy fertilized egg implants in the uterine wall; embryo develops in the uterus

vasectomy the surgical division of the duct in the scrotum that carries sperm

VCF vaginal contraceptive film; a form of contraception consisting of a 2" x 2" thin film laced with spermicide that is inserted into the vagina, where it dissolves, acting as both a physical and chemical barrier

zygote fertilized egg cell

INDEX

Abortion. *See* Birth control
Acquired immune deficiency syndrome. *See* AIDS
Adolescence, 47–48. *See also* Families
  drug abuse during, 97–98
  pregnancy during, 78–80, 102
Adoption. *See also* Children; Families
  agencies, 82
  foreign children and, 82
  natural parents and, 83–84
  reasons for, 81–82
AIDS (acquired immune deficiency syndrome), 55, 93, 97
alcoholism, 40, 95, 97–98
Alzheimer's disease, 40
Amniocentesis, 41. *See also* Birth defects
Ancestor worship, 27
Anna Karenina (Tolstoy), 65
Anorexia nervosa, 95, 97
Artificial insemination, 62. *See* Infertility
Athens, 25

Bank, Stephen B., 66
Barrier contraceptives. *See* Birth control
Belsky, Jay, 91
Beta thalassemia, 40. *See also* Birth defects
Birth control, 28–29
  abortion, 28, 41, 59–61, 78
  abstinence, 53
  barrier methods
    cervical cap, 56–57
    condom, 55
    contraceptive sponge, 57
    diaphragm, 55–56
    intrauterine device, 58
  oral contraceptives
    combination, 53
    ingredients, 53–54
    mechanism, 54
    mini-pill, 53
    morning after pill, 54–55
    multiphasic, 53
    side effects, 54–55
  reasons for not using, 52–53
  rhythm method, 58–59
  spermicides, 55, 57–58
  sterilization, 59
Birth defects, 17–18
  common, 37–40
  counseling, 41–42
  definition, 36–37
  diagnosis, 40–41
Brown, Louise, 62

Cancer
  breast, 40
  colon, 40
Cap. *See* Cervical cap
Census Bureau (U.S.), 15
Center for the Family in Transition, 74
Cervical cap, 55–57. *See also* Birth control
Children. *See also* Families
  abuse of, 93–94
  adoption and, 81–84
  alcoholism and, 95, 97–98
  birth order and, 67
  costs of, 52–53

Index

divorce and, 73, 75–78, 85–88
foster homes and, 84–85
grandparents and, 69
joint custody and, 78
marriage and, 44–45
parental responsibility and, 44–47
reasons for having, 52
rights, 28
siblings and, 66–68
socialization of, 46–47
stepfamilies and, 85–88, 101
teenage parents and, 78–80, 102
working mothers and, 89–92
Chinese, 27–29
Chlamydia, 55
Chorionic villi sampling, 41. *See also* Birth defects
Chromosomes, 34. *See also* Birth defects; Genes
abnormalities of, 37, 39
sex-determining, 35–37
X, 35, 37
Y, 35–37
Clan, 23–24, 28
Color blindness, 36. *See also* Birth defects
Concubine, 24–25, 28
Condom, 55. *See also* Birth control
Contraceptive sponge, 55, 57. *See also* Birth control
Cowan, Carolyn, 44
Cowan, Philip, 44
Cystic fibrosis, 37, 40. *See also* Birth defects

DeFrain, John, 69
Deoxyribonucleic acid. *See* DNA
Diaphragm, 55–56. *See also* Birth control
Divorce. *See also* Children; Families; Stepfamilies
children and, 73, 75–78
economic impact, 74–75
incidence, 73
joint custody and, 78
stepfamilies and, 85–88, 101
DNA (deoxyribonucleic acid), 34, 36. *See also* Birth defects; Chromosomes; Genes

Down's syndrome, 39, 41. *See also* Birth defects
Dynamics. *See* Families, behavior of

Egg, 34–35. *See also* Birth defects
Embryo transfer, 62. *See also* Infertility
Estrogen, 54–55, 63. *See also* Birth control

Faber, Adele, 68
Families. *See also* Children; Divorce; Marriage; Stepfamilies
activities, 71
adolescents and, 47–48, 75–76
adoption, 81–84
alcoholism and, 95, 97–98
American, 29–31
behavior of, 20, 65–72
black, 31, 76–77, 80
blended, 16, 85–88
changes in traditional, 21–22, 73–74, 76–78, 89–92, 99–104
children and, 44–47, 66–68
Chinese, 27–29
conjugal, 15–16
definitions of, 13–16
divorce and, 21, 26, 28, 31, 44, 66, 73–78, 85–88, 101
drug abuse and, 97–98
egalitarian, 16, 30
elderly and, 49–50, 69
emotions and, 18
ethnic influences, 16
extended, 15–16, 24, 26, 30
functions, 14–15, 18–19
genetics and, 17–18, 33–41
grandparents and, 49–50, 69
gratification and, 18–19
Greek, 16, 24–25
Hebrew, 16, 23–24
Hispanic, 31–32
history, 16, 23–32
homosexuality and, 92–93
identity and, 19, 43
illness and, 96–97
incest and, 17–18, 95
independence and, 43–44, 47–48
Iroquois, 16

115

legitimacy and, 17
life cycle, 43–50
marriage and, 15–16, 21, 24–26, 28, 30, 32, 44
matriarchal, 16
matrilineal, 16
medieval, 26
middle age and, 48–49
nuclear, 15–16, 21, 26
one-child, 66
patriarchal, 16, 24–27, 31–32
physical abuse in, 20, 93–94
psychological abuse in, 20, 93
reconstituted, 16
relationships within, 13–16
religion and, 31–32
Roman, 16, 25–26
security and, 18, 27, 47
sexual behavior and, 17–18, 92–93
single-parent, 15, 73, 76–78
socialization and, 18, 46–47
spouse abuse in, 93
status and, 19
successful, qualities of, 69–70, 87–88
theories of, 20
therapy, 65, 70, 72, 94, 96, 98
values and, 19, 46
women, role of, 16, 21, 24, 26, 31, 89–92
working mothers and, 89–92
worldwide trends, 102–4
Family of orientation, 15. *See also* Families
Family of procreation, 15. *See also* Families
Family planning, 64. *See also* Adoption; Birth control; Infertility
birth control and, 52–61
infertility and, 61–63
reasons for, 51–52
sterilization, 59
FDA. *See* Food and Drug Administration
Federal Bureau of Investigation, 93
Fertility drugs, 63. *See also* Infertility
Foam, 57. *See also* Birth control
Food and Drug Administration (FDA), 56

Fragile X syndrome, 40. *See also* Birth defects

Gamete, 34. *See also* Birth defects
Gamete intra-fallopian transfer (GIFT), 62. *See also* Infertility
Gen, 24
Generation gap, 19
Genes. *See also* Birth defects; Chromosomes
defects, 36–40
definition, 34
dominant, 17, 34, 37
markers for, 40–41
predisposition to disease and, 40
recessive, 17–18, 34, 37
Gentry, 27
GIFT. *See* Gamete intra-fallopian transfer
Greeks, 16, 24–25
Guthrie, Woody, 41

Heart disease, 40. *See also* Birth defects
Hebrews, 16, 23–25
hemoglobin, 38
hemophilia, 18, 40. *See also* Birth defects
Homosexuality, 92–93. *See also* Families
Host uterus, 63. *See also* Infertility
Huntington's chorea, 40–41. *See also* Birth defects
Hysterectomy, 59. *See also* Sterilization

Illegitimacy, 17
Incest, 17–18
Infertility. *See also* Family planning
epidemiology, 61
causes, 61
treatment, 62–63
Intrauterine device (IUD). *See* Birth control
In vitro fertilization, 62. *See also* Infertility
Iroquois, 16
IUD. *See* Birth control

Index

Kahn, Michael D., 66

Legitimacy, 17
Leonard, John, 88

Machismo, 31
Manic depression, 40. *See also* Birth defects
Mao Zedong, 28
Marriage. *See also* Children; Divorce; Families
  adjustments in, 44
  arranged, 24–26, 28, 30
  children and, 44–47
  common law, 30
  elderly and, 49–50
  identity and, 43
  independence and, 43–44
Matriarchy, 16
Mazlish, Elaine, 68
Mead, Margaret, 14, 104
Menarche, 80
Menstrual cycle, 54. *See also* Birth control
Miscarriage, 37, 41
Monogamy, 25, 28
Mother Care/Other Care (Scarr), 90
Muscular dystrophy, 37, 40. *See also* Birth defects

National Committee for Adoption, 82. *See also* Adoption
National Council on Child Abuse and Neglect, 93
National Institute of Child Health and Development, 80
Nonoxynol-9, 55, 57. *See also* Birth control

Our Endangered Children (Packard), 86
Ovulation, 54. *See also* Birth control

Packard, Vance, 86
Patriarchy, 16, 25
Pelvic inflammatory disease (PID), 58. *See also* Infertility
Phenylalanine, 38

Phenylketonuria (PKU), 38–39. *See also* Birth defects
PID. *See* Pelvic inflammatory disease
PKU. *See* phenylketonuria
Polycystic kidney disease, 40. *See also* Birth defects
Polygamy, 24
Princeton Center for Infancy, 81
Progestasert, 58. *See also* Birth control
Progesterone, 54
Progestin, 54–55. *See also* Birth control

Relationships. *See* Families
Romanov, house of, 18
Romans, 16, 25–26

Scarr, Sandra, 90
Schizophrenia, 40. *See also* Birth defects
Secrets of Strong Families (Stinnett and DeFrain), 69
Sib, 23
Sibling Bond, The (Bank and Kahn), 66
Siblings, 66–68. *See also* Children
  rivalry, 68, 70
Siblings Without Rivalry (Faber and Mazlish), 68
Sickle cell anemia, 38, 40. *See also* Birth defects
Sparta, 25
Sperm, 34–35
Sponge. *See* Contraceptive sponge
Stepfamilies, 85–88, 101. *See also* Children; Divorce; Families, blended
Stepfamily Foundation of America, 87
Sterilization, 59. *See also* Birth control; Family planning
Stinnett, Nick, 69
Stroke, 40. *See also* Birth defects
Surrogacy, 62–63. *See also* Infertility
Syphilis, 55

Tay-Sachs disease, 38–40. *See also* Birth defects

117

Tolstoy, Leo, 65
Toxic shock syndrome, 57
Trait. *See also* Birth defects; Genes
  dominant, 34
  heterozygous, 34
  homozygous, 34
  male, 35–36
  male-linked, 36
  recessive, 34, 37
Tribe, 23
Tsu, 28

Tubal ligation, 59. *See also* Sterilization

Vaginal contraceptive film, 57–58. *See also* Birth control
Vasectomy, 59. *See also* Sterilization
Verbrugge, Lois, 90

Wallerstein, Judith, 74

Zygote, 35

PICTURE CREDITS

Anderson/Gamma-Liaison: p. 27; AP/Wide World Photos: pp. 35, 36, 38, 39, 51, 60, 63, 74, 83, 84, 91, 94, 103; The Bettmann Archive: pp. 15, 24, 25, 43; Solomon D. Butcher Collection/Nebraska State Historical Society: pp. 23, 29; Charles Campbell/Taurus Photos: p. 65; Laimute Druskis/Taurus Photos: pp. 71, 87, 90; Emerson Teenage Parent Program of the Jefferson County Public School System: p. 79; Spencer Grant/Taurus Photos: p. 97; Hemsey/Gamma-Liaison: p. 56; Eric Kroll/Taurus Photos: pp. 68, 89, 96; Joan Menschenfreund/Taurus Photos: p. 20; The Metropolitan Museum of Art, Gift of Frederic H. Hatch, 1926: cover; Bill Owens: pp. 13, 14, 17, 45; Marilyn Pfaltz/Taurus Photos: p. 81; Martin M. Rotker/Taurus Photos: p. 34; Frank Siteman/Taurus Photos: pp. 48, 53, 73; Ira N. Toff: p. 100; UPI/Bettmann Newsphotos: p. 30; Shirley Zeiberg/Taurus Photos: pp. 46, 47, 67, 99; Original illustrations by Bruce Waldman: pp. 19, 77

Dianne Hales is the author or coauthor of nine books, including *Case Histories* in Chelsea House's ENCYCLOPEDIA OF PSYCHOACTIVE DRUGS, *An Invitation to Health: Your Personal Responsibility, The U.S. Army Total Fitness Program, The Complete Book of Sleep,* and *New Hope for Problem Pregnancies.* She is a contributing editor of *American Health* magazine and a frequent contributor to other magazines, including *McCall's, Redbook,* and *Parade.* Ms. Hales has also written for the *Washington Post,* the *New York Times, American Medical News, Medical World News,* and *Psychiatric News.*

Dale C. Garell, M.D., is medical director of California Childrens Services, Department of Health Services, County of Los Angeles. He is also clinical professor in the Department of Pediatrics and Family Medicine at the University of Southern California School of Medicine and Visiting associate clinical professor of maternal and child health at the University of Hawaii School of Public Health. From 1963 to 1974, he was medical director of the Division of Adolescent Medicine at Children's Hospital in Los Angeles. Dr. Garell has served as president of the Society for Adolescent Medicine, chairman of the youth committee of the American Academy of Pediatrics, and as a forum member of the White House Conference on Children (1970) and White House Conference on Youth (1971). He has also been a member of the editorial board of the *American Journal of Diseases of Children.*

C. Everett Koop, M.D., Sc.D., is Surgeon General, Deputy Assistant Secretary for Health, and Director of the Office of International Health of the U.S. Public Health Service. A pediatric surgeon with an international reputation, he was previously surgeon-in-chief of Children's Hospital of Philadelphia and professor of pediatric surgery and pediatrics at the University of Pennsylvania. Dr. Koop is the author of more than 175 articles and books on the practice of medicine. He has served as surgery editor of the *Journal of Clinical Pediatrics* and editor-in-chief of the *Journal of Pediatric Surgery.* Dr. Koop has received nine honorary degrees and numerous other awards, including the Denis Brown Gold Medal of the British Association of Paediatric Surgeons, the William E. Ladd Gold Medal of the American Academy of Pediatrics, and the Copernicus Medal of the Surgical Society of Poland. He is a Chevalier of the French Legion of Honor and a member of the Royal College of Surgeons, London.